GUITARIST'S GUIDE TO
MUSIC READING

BY
CHRIS BUONO

ISBN 978-1-4584-1143-3

HAL•LEONARD®
CORPORATION
7777 W. BLUEMOUND RD. P.O. BOX 13819 MILWAUKEE, WI 53213

In Australia Contact:
Hal Leonard Australia Pty. Ltd.
4 Lentara Court
Cheltenham, Victoria, 3192 Australia
Email: ausadmin@halleonard.com.au

Visit Hal Leonard Online at
www.halleonard.com

Foreword

The unsung heroes of Hollywood's big action blockbusters are its stuntmen; those daring and tenacious, fastidiously prepared, and very talented individuals who sit in for Pitt, Clooney, or Cruise when it gets hairy and dangerous.

We have "stunt guitarists" in the music education business as well. They may not risk their lives on a daily basis, but they are just as daring, tenacious, fastidious, and talented in their pursuit of perfection while researching, practicing, and then presenting a curriculum on a particular artist, style, or technique.

Hollywood has its Vic Armstrong. The music education biz has its Chris Buono.

Chris was in the process of moving from Boston, where he was teaching at Berklee, when he first rang me up to introduce himself and let me know he would be available for freelance work after the move. Chris' reputation preceded him quite nicely and so we gave him a monster rhythm guitar course project right off the bat. He not only nailed the project on deadline (rare in this biz), but also exceeded all of our expectations with respect to content and presentation (even rarer).

Over the following months, Chris delivered a dozen more projects for TrueFire, covering everything from funk to fusion, blues to rock, heavy metal to shred, modal improvisation to guitar part arranging. Whatever we threw at him he nailed with the same tenacity, quality, and professionalism as the first project.

How he managed to balance his teaching, performing, and authoring while being such a supportive husband and doting father is in itself an amazing accomplishment, deserving of a "duty above and beyond" medal. How he maintained such a positive attitude and somehow kept it all together after hurricane Sandy destroyed his family's home is beyond my capacity to even begin to explain. The cat is extraordinary.

I'm honored to have been asked to write this foreword for a man that I not only respect professionally, but also revere personally. I'm also honored to welcome you to this extraordinary learning experience.

Every guitarist that doesn't already know how to read music, yearns to learn how. That's why you've picked up this book. And that's why Chris authored it. Without a shadow of a doubt, I can assure you that you're in the right place, at the right time, with the right teacher—scratch that, the perfect teacher.

Now grab your guitar, find a quiet corner in the shed, and get to work!

Brad Wendkos

Founder & CEO - TrueFire

Contents

Chapter 7: Essential Notation Components, Part 1

Chapter 8: Essential Notation Components, Part 2

Chapter 9: Reading by Degree

Chapter 10: Essential Notation Components, Part 3

Chapter 11: Establishing Rhythm Recognition Skills | The Power of the Triplet

Chapter 12: Next Level Time Signatures

Introduction

If you're reading this book you probably think reading standard notation on guitar is hard. And it is—to an extent. I was just like you; I tried for years to read, only to fail time and time again. Perhaps you tried to make it happen here and there and, for whatever reason, it just didn't click. Or maybe you turned to one of the iconic beginner method books or tried reading down chart after chart cold because someone told you to do so. Frustratingly, you more than likely butchered the tunes along the way and never actually made it to the end. Perhaps when the time came for you to read something with advance notice, you spent hours dissecting and memorizing the piece, which resulted in you never really reading at all. And, even after all that work, you barely knew what it is you were playing and would have been in big trouble if even the slightest change were made. It's OK, you're not alone—not even close.

To effectively remedy the situation, *The Guitarist's Guide to Music Reading | Bridging the Gap Between the Neck and Notation* will present you with a new approach to learning to read on guitar. It's a combination of time-tested concepts that are based on dealing with two elements that I think are the guitar-reading elephants in the room: Not enough opportunity and lack of neck vision. These points and more will be addressed in the following sections and drilled ad nauseam throughout the book. With ample time and effort, this book will garner results. So, enjoy the ride as you begin to finally learn to read music on guitar.

The Approach

When we were kids learning to read words, we started in small chunks and built from there. The process involved repetition of these chunks until we knew them cold. Our teachers provided lots of opportunities for our developing skills to be molded and sharpened. Reading music should be approached in much the same way. So much so it should seem elementary and, frankly, almost too easy. That being said, don't think of your work in this book as "easy," but rather "at ease." We will go through the basics and really get to know them through constant and plentiful application; that is, lots and lots of opportunities to, well, read!

Naysayers often point their finger at tablature as the reason why we six-stringers can't read. While that ingenious device makes it easy to learn your favorite song or lick quickly, it's not one that just popped out of nowhere, and neither did the plight of guitarists with dysfunctional reading skills. Want to know one of the biggest, if not *the* biggest, reasons why guitarists generally can't read? The guitar has more than one way to play the same pitch, and in many cases, guitarists don't know where to start. As you go through the concepts and read the gaggle of passages throughout this book, you'll be constantly exploring neck vision concepts that address this issue. So much so that by the end of the book you should feel like a neck-vision ninja.

Here are the concepts that make up the core of my approach and methodology. Read it carefully and then be ready to dig in!

Starting Small, Going Slow

In order to effectively learn to read music, you have to initially approach it slowly in small steps and work at it a lot. The following concepts support this simple mantra, but it's up to you to actually put them into practice (if there were any other way this book would be all about it, trust me). Doing so will require discipline, desire, and a lot of heart. You can already play and at times it will seem frustrating to be reading what seems like prenatal-level, nonsensical melodies. But, if you want to do this—and I mean *really* do this—you'll need to accept the following truths and seize every reading opportunity you can, as well as create your own.

Gradual Concept Learning

Learning to read music, especially on the guitar, needs to happen gradually. Like the written word, there are many, many components to written music. Each concept *must* be thoroughly explored one at a time before moving onto the next. And as you progress, it's extremely helpful when the music has a logical flow, as every last passage does throughout this book. Whatever you read in one line will carry over to the next one and so on. This is a great way to take it all in and really get a handle on reading on guitar. With that in mind, be aware that this book will constantly encourage you to further delve into whatever it is you're learning on your own by writing similar passages, thus giving you more opportunity to read. In the end, you'll want to find and create as many ways possible to build on each reading concept.

Developing "Recognition and Reaction" Skills

As you read the text in this book, you are immediately able to recognize and react to the words on the paper. You know their definitions, the proper pronunciation, and their syntax—all that good grammatical stuff. As a result, there's a logical flow. You attained these *recognition and reaction* skills through gradual learning and lots of mental elbow grease. The same applies to learning how to read music. The goal is to come upon a chart or lead sheet and not experience any hesitation. Through gradual learning you can attain the needed recognition and reaction skills to do so.

Focused Note Groups and Passages

A key component to this entire approach, especially the recognition and reaction part, is reading in pre-defined, focused groups of notes. You'll find groups with as few as three notes all the way up to ones built from seven-tone scales. In these early stages, a vital key is to know your parameters. These *Note Groups* will be written in two-, four-, and sometimes eight-bar *passages*. Let's not think of them in the more commonly used terminology—"exercises" or "drills"—as those words imply that these music-reading passages should be played over and over again. That's not the case at all, which brings us to the concept of …

Fresh Material

Another vital piece of the sight-reading puzzle is reading as much *fresh* material as possible. It directly addresses the attempt to not memorize whatever you're trying to read. To do that, you need to read in small, focused Note Groups as much as you can. This is yet another reason why I strongly urge you to write your own passages once you complete a section or chapter. At the same time, you'll see there will be more than meets the eye in the passages provided in this book through various recycling concepts explained later.

Importance of Slight Variations

To create vats of fresh material, the passages will contain slight note variation and so should any passages you compose on your own. For example, it could be gradual pitch re-ordering or acute note value changes through an extended series of passages. Whatever the approach, slight variations allow you the same advantages that focused note groups afford, which is having a handle on the passages' parameters, while at the same time providing the much-needed fresh material. In essence, when you know what's coming, you read with more confidence. That allows you to relax and learn to read at ease instead of with stress.

Attack First, Sustain Later

To start things off I'll introduce rhythm-only reading concepts that focus on the most basic attribute of rhythm—where in time do you attack (pick) the note. You'll explore this by literally *tapping out the rhythms*. After that skill begins to develop and strengthen, you'll then start to play and sustain pitches for their intended durations. Splitting up the two main components of music like this starts you off on the right foot and helps build a strong foundation on which you continue to build in bite-size chunks. Then, as these chunks become bigger and bigger, they're preparing you to read extended pieces more effectively.

Constant Shifting

To directly address the multiple locations of the same pitch (unisons) that can be played on the guitar, you'll be directed to shift each Note Group or Passage you're reading to every possible neck position. You'll even shift up and/or down an octave, as there will be plenty of occasions where you'll be asked to do just that. While some of these positions may not be where you'll settle on reading melodies as a norm, it's still beneficial for you to do so at this stage, as it has many added benefits beyond just reading.

The idea is to use these concepts to develop ninja-level neck awareness skills, which will improve not only your reading ability, but every aspect of playing the guitar.

Diagonal Movements

Due to the architecture of the guitar and standard tuning, you don't have to go far to play the same pitch on different strings. This creates multiple ways to play the same note in the same pitch range. This will be the first level of shifting, which guides the next level as well as fosters the ability to shift when the melody demands a specific range that can only be played in certain areas of the neck. Building skill in the latter will ease the stress of reading when you come up on seemingly difficult passages that can't be read in whatever position you're currently playing.

Unison Position Shifts

The next level of shifting will have you making what I call *unison position shifts*. When using diagonal movements, you'll learn the various positions in which a three-note melody can be read. This skill not only multiplies the ways in which you can read the notes, but also helps to build what will become a supreme awareness of where to read a melody on your axe.

G–B String Awareness

Throughout your shifting of note locations, whether it be within a diagonal movement or a unison position shift, you'll need to be aware of the half-step tuning difference between the third and second strings as compared to the other adjacent string pairs. This plays a big part in fingering differences, not to mention in confusing the would-be six-string reader. The more time you challenge yourself with this anomaly in regards to shifting, the easier it will become to read with ease.

Octave Shifts

There will be many times that you'll be asked to play an octave higher than what's written, and occasionally an octave lower. Both instances occur often enough to require you to work on this skill, and both require *octave shifts*, a type of shifting you'll learn about and work on as you progress.

Recycling Passages

While it may look as if there's an endless array of passages throughout this book, an ample reader can blow through them all in no time flat. With dedicated practice, you'll also be there soon enough, and that's why it's important to hip you to the many ways you can recycle both the passages in this book and any that you write on your own. For starters, you could shift every last passage up and/or down an octave as introduced in the previous section. But there's more than meets the eye here—a *lot* more.

Reading Upside Down

The most obvious way to recycle a page full of passages is to literally turn the book or sheet upside down. That's right, you'll be asked to take this book off the music stand, turn it upside down, and read it again.

Reading in Columns

You'll notice there are myriad pages containing only reading passages with no text in sight. These pages will have passages aligned in a way where you can read vertically down the page in columns. For instance you can start at the top of a page and read only the first bar of each passage or vice versa.

Streaming

Instead of adhering to the double bar line that indicates the end of a passage, you could keep going and stream all the passages on one page together. Then turn it upside down and do it again.

Reading Across Even or Odd Pages

You could once again disregard double bar lines and read straight across an even number page to its horizontally corresponding odd numbered page. While you're at it, turn the page upside down and repeat the reading. See where this is going?

The next three recycling methods are a bit more advanced concepts that garner skills beyond just reading. Have patience, as they will take time to implement. But don't give up, as they will be worth their weight in gold and then some.

Counting It Out

In Chapters 2 and 5 you'll work on your rhythm recognition skills. After you complete the collections of four-bar passages, you'll learn about counting methods where you'll be directed to go back and call out the beats as you read. This is a great way to strengthen your grip on meter and your overall placement within whatever it is you're reading.

Transposing

In Chapter 11 you'll learn how to transpose, which in this case means you'll be reading what's written in a different key. Sounds hard, and at first it may seem that way, until you get a hold of the intervallic concepts presented later in the book. Once those are in place, you can go back and recycle your book 11 times! And, that's not counting following through with flipping over the book, reading in columns, streaming, reading horizontally across even and odd numbered pages, or reading with a backbeat pulse feel.

Like I said—a lot more than meets the eye.

Added Benefits

Putting the aforementioned concepts and approaches into practice will not only help you become a great reader, but in time will have these added benefits.

Transposition Skills

Being able to transpose what's written goes far beyond recycling your reading books. Having the ability to shift keys on the fly will have incredibly positive effects on your improvisation skills especially when it comes to blowing over changes.

Interval Study: Reading by Note and Number

Transposing requires you to have a keen awareness of intervals, thus allowing you to read a melody by note number, or degree. That type of knowledge is the cornerstone of music theory and will be of use to you in just about everything you do musically.

Enhanced Improvisation Tools (Rhythm Reading Only)

Speaking of improving your improvisational skills, the ability to quickly read just rhythms gives you a great way to easily digest new rhythmic figures that can be applied to any tired licks you may have in your arsenal.

Confidence

Finally, having solid reading skills changes your overall confidence level. Now you can learn more music faster, play more music on the fly with other musicians, take on gigs you wouldn't otherwise consider, write out your ideas, be able to communicate them faster—the list goes on and on. In the end, it equals a completely different guitarist.

DVD

You'll find every last passage recorded on the DVD that comes with this book. The example numbers seen in the charts will correspond with the files found on the disc. At the start of each track will be a one-bar count-in shouted out by yours truly. Unless otherwise indicated, following the suggested 50–65 bpm tempo range seen throughout most of the book, you'll hear the tracks at four different tempos: Passages with no subdivisions will be played at 65 bpm, passages that include eighth notes will be played at 60 bpm, passages that include eighth-note triplets and quarter-note triplets will be played at 55 bpm, and finally passages that include sixteenth notes and sixteenth-note triplets will be played 50 bpm. In Chapter 10, passages 485–504 were all played at 65 bpm, as were passages 649–660 in Chapter 12.

To get the most out of your efforts, make the use of these recordings your last resort. The goal here is to read, not mimic or memorize!

Reading Truths Revealed

Before you dive into the book, I want to point out a few truths that may help ease the tension associated with reading music on guitar and help you start to develop your confidence. First, when approaching a chart that may have just been put in front of you, keep in mind that even the best readers will give it a "once over." As you "reference read," look for spots in the chart where you'll need to shift positions, deal with wide intervals, change keys and/or meters, or whatever else might be a potential bump in the road as you "read it down." Don't hesitate to take out a pencil or highlighter to, well, highlight whatever anomalies you discover. (Just don't forget to pack a pencil or highlighter in your gig bag!)

More often than not, when given a chart to read down for the first time, you'll be able to approach it as more of a reference tool. You'll have the freedom to interpret a written melody or freely comp a chord progression. In fact, there will be times you'll be *expected* to do this, which is a skill in itself. The point is, the anxiety many guitarists experience is sometimes for naught, as things are sometimes not as strict as you think. And, when a chart *does* need to be read down to the letter, remember that you're often given the music in advance.

These truths are in no way meant to lead you to believe that everything in music is lackadaisical. Reading music comes in many forms for a guitarist, especially if you're playing in styles that contain varying degrees of improvisation. Sure, there exist scenarios where a lethal sight-reader of the highest order is needed to do the job, and there are those who can read down just about anything on sight. Just know that these are rare instances and ones that will not likely just fall in your lap unless you put yourself out there. However, in my nearly quarter of a century playing the guitar professionally—which has included everything from record dates to touring to pit bands to last minute wedding gigs and more—it's not at all common for a chart to be thrown in front of me on the spot. When it does happen, they're not nearly as difficult as most guitarists fear them to be.

In the end, I sincerely hope this book serves as a spark for you to become a proficient reader, so you can make playing music that much more fulfilling. It's an incredible skill that never stops giving back.

You can do this. Ready to learn how?

About the Author

Hailed as a "multi-media guitar madman," Chris Buono infiltrates the modern guitar world from myriad directions. Be it on CD, in video, in the minds of gear aficionados, or in book form, his reach is vast. At the forefront is Buono's passion for conveying knowledge to those who are willing to work for it. Through over 20 years of teaching in just about every forum a guitarist can, including five years as a professor in the esteemed Guitar Department at Berklee College of Music and currently as a prolific TrueFire artist, Chris Buono has helped propel students from all over the world to new heights.

To learn more about Chris, visit his official web site: *www.chrisbuono.com*.

You can also catch up with him on various social media outlets, as listed below:

http://www.facebook.com/pages/Chris-Buono/179100172190
http://twitter.com/#!/ChrisBuono
http://www.youtube.com/user/chrisbuonovideos?feature=mhum

Dedication

For my "alpha" cousin Louellen Renda. You made every moment I ever spent with you the very best it could be.

To the "crazy old uncle" that came to live with us: You changed everything and showed us what it is to love unconditionally. Thanks, Hunter. We loved you just as much, puppy. Say hello to Murphy, Broka, Fat, and Jesse for us.

Acknowledgments

Always, the deepest thanks goes to my wonderful family: My lifelong love, Stacy, and my two boys, John and Wil. Thanks to Jeff Schroedl for taking this project on and being a man of great patience. Longtime thanks to Frankie Cicala for teaching me how to read, to Vic Juris for showing me how important it is to read, to Gerry Carboy, Dave Fiuczynski, and Wayne Krantz for helping me see the big picture, and to Mick Goodrick for setting the bar so high. Perpetual thanks and much respect to Michael Mueller, Adam Perlmutter, Mac Randall, Chris O'Byrne, Michael Ross, Michael Molenda, and Jude Gold for all of the opportunities and guidance over the years. Finally, enormous thanks go to Andrew Pevny for his exhaustive work on the hundreds of passages throughout this book.

CHAPTER 1

Getting Started

To begin getting your reading skills together, it's important to start with the basic components of music notation. This chapter presents essential core musical concepts that directly pertain to reading as well as foundational notation symbols. While there's much more coming your way in this book, and even more for you to learn about after you've completed it, remember it all starts with these basics, so read carefully and come back to this chapter whenever necessary. The goal here is to keep the amount of content you need to get started to a bare minimum. That way you won't get bogged down with too many notation components while you begin building your basic reading skills.

Two Basic Elements

Music is broken down into two basic components: Rhythm and pitch. Proficiency in reading requires simultaneous mastery of both. But to *begin* building your reading skills, we'll examine them separately. Chapter 2 starts you off with reading rhythm-only passages. In Chapter 3, we'll get into reading pitch. To prepare for what's to come, let's be sure you know what's what in regards to these two elements.

Rhythm

A simple definition of rhythm is the motion of music through time. For our purposes, it's important you clearly understand its core components, explained below, as these will be used throughout the book and should be part of your own core understanding of rhythm and music as a whole.

As music moves through time, regular or consistent *pulsations* occur. These pulses are more commonly known as *beats*. It is these beats that determine when to attack a note and how long to hold it. Although beats generally divide time into equal portions, some are felt more strongly than others by way of stress. Strong beats are often referred to as *downbeats* and are followed by weaker beats. These successions of strong and weak beats occur over time and thus form patterns, which in turn make music tangible, with regard to time. Furthermore, these beats may be split into halves, thirds, quarters, or other *subdivisions*.

The organization of beats into a pattern, according to stress, is called *meter*. The rate of speed at which these patterns of beats occur is called the *tempo*, which is measured in *beats per minute*, which is typically abbreviated as "bpm." The tempo is indicated at the beginning of the piece by a *tempo marking*, which is found above the staff, on the left.

Pitch

The actual sounds we make within the realm of rhythm are called tones, which have a relative highness and lowness. This relativity is called *pitch*. It's that simple.

The Staff, Clef Signs, and Signatures

Music notation symbols are placed on a *staff*, which consists of five parallel lines and their four intervening spaces.

Together with other notation elements, basic symbols that represent rhythm and pitch—the notes—are placed on those lines and spaces (and extensions thereof), making up the music you're about to learn to read. The type of note conveys not only *where* in time it should be played but also its duration, or how long it should ring. The note's position on the staff, be it on a line or space, conveys its pitch.

The lines and spaces are to be counted starting from the bottom as seen above.

On the leftmost side of a staff will be a *clef* sign, which is used at the beginning of a staff to identify pitch range.

This one is called the *treble* or *G clef*. Its name indicates the pitch name G is to be assigned to the second line. Upon close inspection you can see this is depicted in the clef itself. At four different junctures the treble clef intersects this second line, which is the only time this happens (making it somewhat obvious something is up)—more on that in the next section.

To the right of the staff will be two important notation elements: The *key* and *time* signatures.

The *key signature* determines the tonal or key center of a given piece of music. It will contain a set of accidentals—either *sharp* symbols (♯) or *flat* symbols (♭)—unique to the given key, whether major or minor. Key signatures simplify notation by displaying the required accidentals after the clef sign, thus eliminating the need to litter them on the staff throughout the piece.

The time signature will be displayed as two stacked numbers, which determine the meter (top number) and note duration (bottom number), as well as beat type (discussed in detail later in the book). It will always appear at the beginning of a piece and wherever a meter change may occur within the piece.

Notes

As mentioned earlier, the treble, or G, clef indicates that the second line from the bottom is a G note. With that in mind you can logically see how the rest of the notes on the staff are assigned.

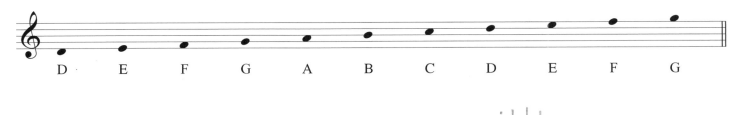

Conventional music pedagogy is quick to call out traditional mnemonic devices like *Every Good Boy Deserves Fudge*, to help memorize the notes on the lines, and **FACE** for the notes in the spaces—but there's a much more applicable connection. Music notes are named by letter, in alphabetical order, from A to G, and then repeated. The staff then also works in alphabetical order, starting with D in the space directly below the first line and then following a line-space-line-space pattern all the way up to G, in the space directly above the fifth, or top, line. This simple staff attribute is the key to putting the puzzle together "on paper" and how this book will present reading music on guitar.

Throughout the book we'll deal with five essential note types:

| **Whole note** | **Half note** | **Quarter note** | **Eighth note** | **Sixteenth note** |

While these are by far the most common, you'll encounter others as you get more into reading. For now, though, this is the essential set with which to start and is what you'll see most often in guitar music.

The bottom number of the time signature (called the *beat unit*) is what determines note *duration*, as measured in beats. Since 4/4 is by far the most common time signature in Western music, it's customary to learn how to read rhythms in that "common" time. When a "4" is on the bottom of a time signature, the note duration hierarchy will be as follows:

Whole note = 4 beats

Half note = 2 beats

Quarter note = 1 beat

Eighth note = 1/2 beat

Sixteenth note = 1/4 beat

The system is set up so the beat unit's note duration value is always one beat. In 4/4 time, that's the quarter note, which is considered the universal beat unit. In fact, most musicians assume the duration hierarchy shown above unless otherwise noted. From there the duration hierarchy is set up in multiples of two. Any notes' value greater than the beat unit is a product of multiplying by two and any notes' value less than the beat unit is a product of dividing by two. Simple math here, folks.

The only possible beat unit number (bottom number of the time signature) candidates you need to be aware of are 2, 4, 8, and 16. Memorizing all the corresponding note symbols to their beat unit number counterparts is as easy as associating the number to the name. Like this: 2 = half note, 4 = quarter note, 8 = eighth note, 16 = sixteenth note. While there are technically other possible beat units, they're rarely employed and you need not burden yourself with them at this stage.

Contrary to conventional wisdom, another way to approach the note duration hierarchy is to assign the bottom number of a time signature to the value of the whole note. From there you simply divide by two as you successively go down the line. For example, if you have an 8 on the bottom of a time signature, the beat unit is an eighth note (the second most common beat unit). After doing the simple math described earlier you'll come up with the following:

Whole note = 8 beats

Half note = 4 beats

Quarter note = 2 beats

Eighth note = 1 beat

Sixteenth note = 1/2 beat

To review: Assign the bottom number of a time signature to the value of the whole note and then divide by two as you go down. Some might find it easier to realize the values of the other notes.

Rests

Music is not only made of sound and where it's played against a consistent pulse, but it also contains periods of silence. These moments are represented by symbols called *rests*.

| **Whole rest** | **Half rest** | **Quarter rest** | **Eighth rest** | **Sixteenth rest** |

Rests follow all the same rules in regards to duration as their corresponding notes do according to the beat unit rules discussed earlier; for example, in 4/4 time, a whole rest is four beats of silence.

Bar Lines and Repeat Signs

You've learned that rhythm is felt in patterns. These patterns are made up of strong beats followed by a consistent number of weak beats. Every time one of these patterns occur, we call it a *bar* or *measure* of music. To convey those divisions in notation we use bar lines—vertical lines laid over the staff lines in perpendicular fashion.

There are several types of bar lines, but you only need to understand three in the beginning stages of reading. The *single* bar line separates groups of beats. The thin, *double* bar lines indicate the end of a section. The final double bar lines, comprising one thin and one thick line, indicate the end of a piece. This is known as *fine* (Italian for "end").

In addition to the three basic bar lines, you will soon work with another type of music bar separator called a *repeat sign*.

As you may have guessed, a repeat sign instructs you to do exactly what its name says. We'll go over repeat signs in greater detail in Chapter 10.

Reading Mantras

Starting in the next chapter, you're going to read—a *lot*. Keep these three simple reading mantras in your head as make your way through the book (and beyond), and you'll become a great reader.

- **Always read with a metronome.** All that you've read about rhythm thus far has made mention of consistent pulsations, or beats. It's important to read music with a beat sounding in the background so that you're learning how to play the correct note durations. The easiest way to do this is to use a metronome—be it a hardware unit or a software application on your computer, phone, or tablet. Set your metronome to the tempo marking at the start of each piece. The last thing you want to do is read with rhythmic blindness—especially considering the next chapter's focus: Rhythm!

- **Always read ahead.** You should never be reading the note you're actually playing. As you play one note, you should be looking ahead to at least the next note, if not the one after that. Your goal is eventually to read entire measures ahead. This is absolutely essential to becoming a proficient reader.

- **Don't stop**. If you make a mistake while reading, *don't stop*. Get into this habit right from the start. Look at it this way: If you make a mistake and then you try to "go back" and play it right, you're just playing the supposed right note out of time. So, you're still wrong. The better way to go is learn to take these mistakes, or "clams," in stride and make it to the end. You'd be surprised how many students would *never* see the end of a piece if I let them.

  This concept goes hand-in-hand with reading ahead. If you're reading ahead and you come upon a note or motif that you can't visualize, then skip it. It's OK. You'll close those gaps as you become a better reader. It's much better to make a minor mistake than make the most colossal of all reading errors—getting lost. Nothing stifles music more than a musician in an ensemble getting lost. It brings everyone down and feels heaviest on the reader who lost his place. We don't want that to be you, OK?

CHAPTER 2

Establishing Rhythm Recognition Skills | Downbeats

In Chapter 1, *Getting Started*, you learned that standard notation effectively conveys two basic principles of music: Rhythm and pitch. Whether reference reading a rehearsed piece of music or sight-reading on the spot, in order to read down a chart you must first develop skills that will allow you to quickly recognize and react to what you're looking at. Starting with rhythm recognition skills, the next two chapters (as well as Chapter 5) will hip you to essential reading techniques that allow you to do just that. Throughout each chapter you'll be introduced to the underlying concepts that make these techniques come to life.

Tapping Out Rhythms

Getting on board with the *attack first, sustain later* approach you'll start to develop your rhythm recognition skills through a technique called "tapping out." For this section there's no guitar needed, so put your dearly beloved aside for now and get your hands ready to react as you'll be literally tapping the rhythms you're reading with your hands. What you tap—your knee, chest, or tabletop—is up to you. The idea here is to focus on one part of the rhythm equation (the attack) and ease into the next part (sustain), allowing you to first approach reading music one step at a time.

Downbeats & Related Rests

The first set of passages contains notes that are to be played on the *downbeat*. This means everything you tap will be in sync with a pulse or beat. Starting with a downbeat-only feel is important since it's much easier to recognize and react to a consistent pulsation through time (i.e., beats) than it is to spaces in between the pulse, which is what is required of you when playing subdivisions of the pulse (introduced in Chapter 5).

The idea of tapping out attacks can be applied to any note type, but for the initial tapping out exercises you will only see whole, half, and quarter notes and their related rests in 4/4. Why? Because in addition to the common use of 4/4, when any one of these note types are played and sustained for their intended durations, they would lead into another downbeat. That makes learning to read a lot simpler in these crucial beginning stages. In regards to their related rests, your next action (attack or following rest) would occur on, you guessed it, a downbeat!

DOWNBEAT SEMANTICS

It's not uncommon to hear the term "downbeat" used to describe the first beat of a bar or even the very first hit of a tune that lands on the first beat. No matter how you slice it, it all comes down to one thing—playing a note or a chord on the beat.

Before you start tapping out the exercises, let's take a quick review of note and rest values when you have a *4* on the bottom of the time signature, thus making the quarter note the beat unit:

Whole note and rest: 4 beats

Half note and rest: 2 beats

Quarter note and rest: 1 beat

As you tap out the exercises keep these three reading mantras in place:

- **Always read with a metronome.** If it's a train wreck and you're thinking you can turn it off "for now," DON'T. Be patient, give yourself a chance, and try slowing down the tempo before you go through the exercises rhythmically blind.

- **Always read ahead.** Take advantage of the beginning four-bar passages that have just whole notes and half notes and rests. Here's where you can tap the downbeat and then immediately look ahead to the next note or rest without having to worry about the duration.

- **Don't stop.** Simple as it sounds, but oh so important. Finish what you start regardless of what reading calamity may be unfolding before eyes. Remember, the goal is to always know where you are no matter what. It's a skill you'll cherish when it really counts.

Ready? Great, let's get to work.

With your metronome set in the indicated tempo range of 50–65 bpm—comfortable enough for you to start looking ahead—tap out the following four sections of four-bar passages.

Whole notes

Half notes

Quarter notes

Mixed Downbeat Notes & Rests

Now that you've tapped out some downbeat-only four-bar passages, remember there are many ways you can recycle them, as discussed in the introduction. For instance, take this book and flip it upside down or simply start from the last note of the last passage and read backwards. Aside from the material presented here, I encourage you to compose your own passages. If you're not sure where to start, base your examples on the ones already here in the book; for example, flip-flop bars 1–2 and 3–4, so that you're reading 2–1–4–3. In the end, it's all about reading fresh material, but in these beginning stages, it's also about reading *related* material.

BONUS!

Tapping out rhythms is much more than an elementary reading exercise; in fact, it's a skill you will find useful even after you've become a proficient reader. For example, it is a great way to prepare for a rhythmically complex chart, especially when you come up against unfamiliar rhythms in your "once over" reviews.

Tapping & Counting It Out

When it comes to building your rhythm recognition skills, there's another important skill you should develop—one that will carry over to everything you read—and that's *counting*. Revisit the passages you just tapped out and, with a metronome, count the meter out loud, "1-2-3-4," as you tap them again. Sounds simple, and it is—for now. But this is just a precursor to counting while tapping subdivisions in Chapter 5. It becomes far more challenging, but even more beneficial.

TAPPING ALTERNATIVES

The physical act of tapping out rhythms can take a toll on your hands as well as on whatever you're tapping if the receiving end is part of your body. This rhythm-only reading can be just as effectively accomplished by playing percussive "scratches" on your guitar (as heard on the audio examples). Simply replace the taps with pick hand strumming across all six strings while damping all six strings with your fret hand.

CHAPTER 3

Establishing Pitch Recognition Skills

Now it's time to bring in the other half of the musical equation: *Pitch*. One of the biggest problems that guitarists face when learning to read music is determining *where* on the neck the notes should be played. Often, the guitarist ends up having to break down and basically memorize the piece, rather than reading it. Here, you'll learn about two essential approaches in regards to neck vision that will help combat this age-old battle.

Note Group 1: B–C–D

To get started, we first need to identify some notes to work with on the neck. As you progress through the various concepts and reading components in this book, you'll learn to read pitch using *note groups*. For the most part, these groups will contain three notes, an intentional organization designed to work within the first two pitch-reading concepts we're going to use—but more on that later.

Note group 1 contains the notes B, C, and D.

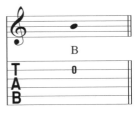 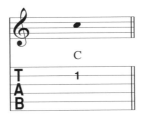 

Note B with Tab   **Note C with Tab**   **Note D with Tab**

Now let's look at them all together on the staff.

Notice the line-space-line pattern the notes follow from B to D. This alphabetical placement is the staff's most basic attribute and the beginning of realizing that reading is not about just seeing one note at a time, but rather a bigger picture.

Using all downstrokes on the second string in open position, play the following passages with your metronome set within the indicated tempo range (50–65 bpm). I encourage you to play one line at a time, stopping at the thin double bar lines, in these beginning stages. After you've played though all of the passages, recycle them at will using the methods described earlier in the book. Be sure to space out your reading sessions, both to avoid the possibility of memorization and to help keep your sanity intact!

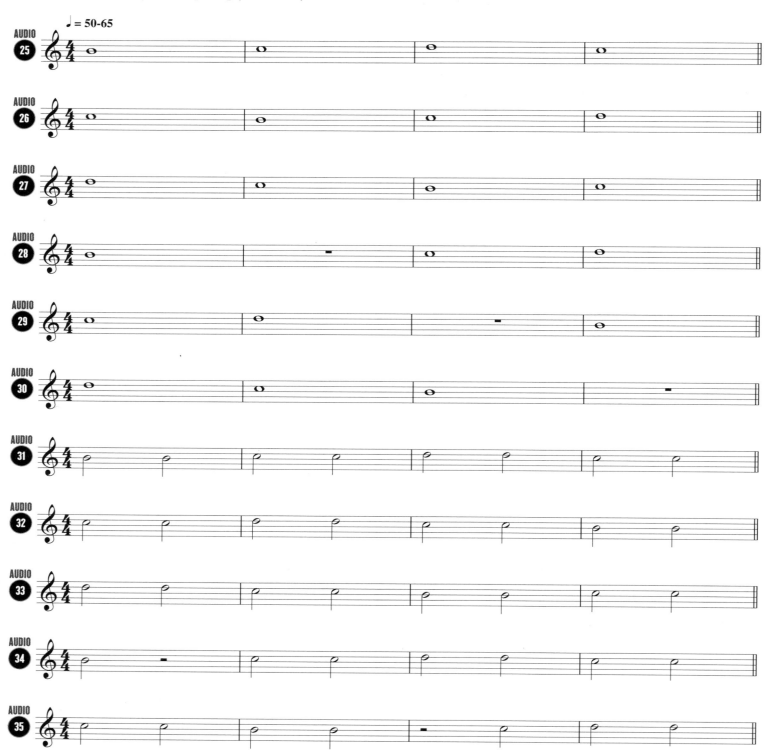

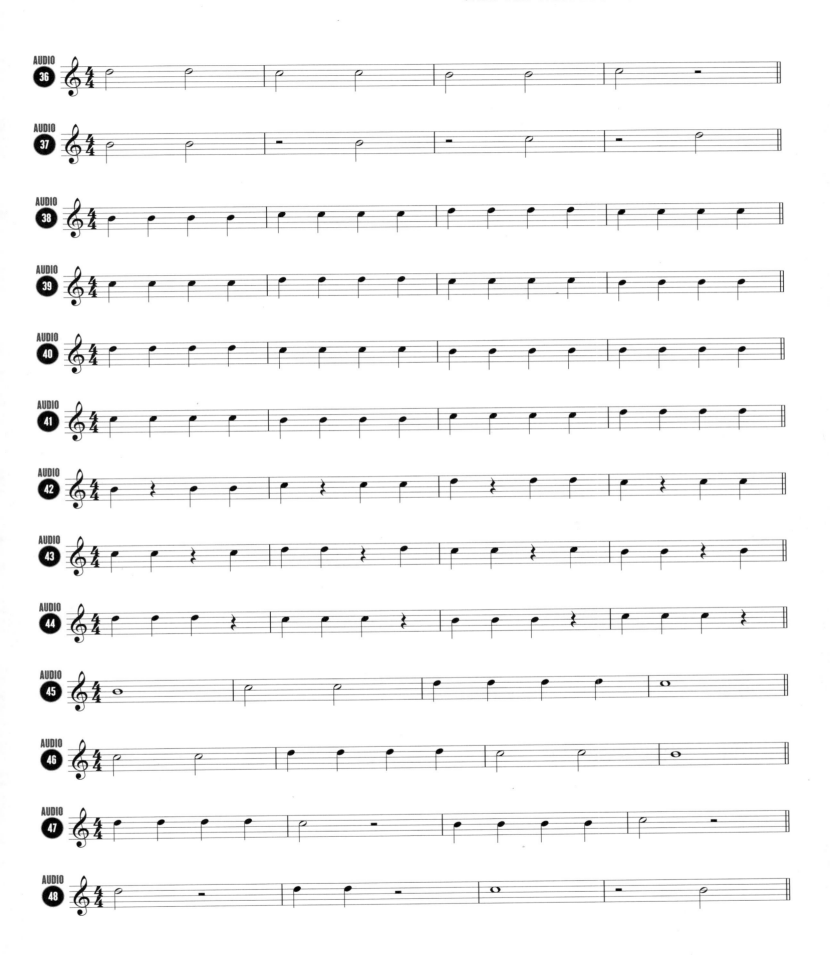

Diagonal Movements

As mentioned earlier, most of the note groups throughout this book are presented in groups of three. Besides putting you at ease by reading in guitar-friendly three-notes-per-string patterns, three-note groups help to convey a vital neck vision concept I call *unison position shifts*. To see how this works, let's first look at something I call *diagonal movements*.

Fact: There's more than one way to play the same note in the same pitch range on your guitar. In fact, some notes have up to five locations across the fretboard. For example, take the C note you just learned to read on the second string, at the first fret. Check out how many ways you can play that same pitch and how those note locations progress up the neck diagonally:

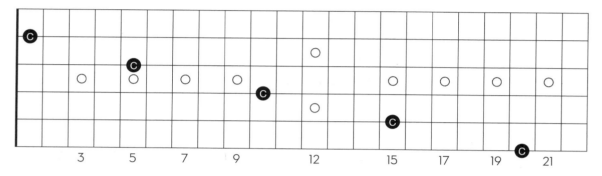

Horizontal neck grid showing locations of "C"

If you're looking down at the guitar, these shifting note locations look as if they're coming up the neck diagonally towards you. Although the tone, or *timbre*, of the note will vary slightly across string and neck locations, it's still the same pitch. Indeed, these five locations of C are all depicted in the same location on the staff—the third space.

As the notes progress diagonally towards you, notice the distance in frets from one adjacent string to the next. With the exception of the second to third string movement (four frets), the notes are separated by five frets (or 2-1/2 steps). This is a positive by-product of standard tuning that allows us to play the myriad chord shapes, scale fingerings, and arpeggio shapes that make our guitar world go 'round. This G–B string awareness will play a key role in fingering differences and you'll have plenty of opportunity to challenge this anomaly when exploring unison position shifts.

Unison Position Shifts

The fact that almost every pitch played on the guitar can be played in more than one location yet be depicted in the same location on the staff is one of the greatest challenges a guitarist faces on the road to functionally reading. One way to overcome that challenge is to tackle it head on, and that's where *unison position shifts* come in. The idea behind this concept is simple: Play every possible fretting sequence within a three-note group by shifting notes to lower (or higher) adjacent strings one note at a time. Sounds complex, but in practice it's both simple *and* effective.

To begin, let's look at Note Group 1 in a single-string horizontal array on the next lower adjacent string from where you first learned it: With B, C, and D set in the 4th position on the 3rd string.

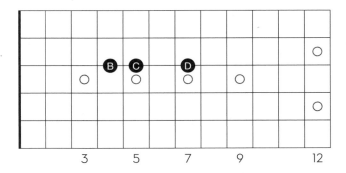

Horizontal neck grid showing 4th position "B-C-D"

If this looks familiar, it means you're starting to see beyond just the notes themselves. Indeed, this is the same horizontal half-step/whole-step vision that was first seen on the 2nd string, except this time the entire Note Group is fretted, as opposed to the lead-off note being open. That being said, another early step in seeing the bigger picture is to not let open strings skew your neck vision. What you played on the 2nd string is identical to what's displayed here on the 3rd string with regard to intervals. Tuck that concept away as it will come back later in the book in a big way.

The idea behind unison position shifts is not to "lift" the entire three-notes-per-string sequence and transplant it as was seemingly done here, but rather to shift the notes one by one to an adjacent string. Using the B–C–D three-notes-per-string sequence in the open position, you would then take the lowest note—the open B—and shift it diagonally towards you to the 4th fret of the 3rd string. The resultant fingering scheme is this 1st-position array.

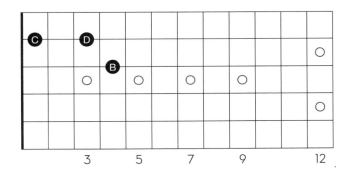

Horizontal neck grid showing 1st position "C-D-B"

Since the shifted notes are still the same pitch range, the distance from the original location to the new location is called a unison interval; hence the name *unison* position shifts. Continuing to move from the 1st-position array, you then make another diagonal unison shift, this time shifting the 1st-fret C to its unison counterpart at the 5th fret of the 3rd string, thus creating a 3rd-position array.

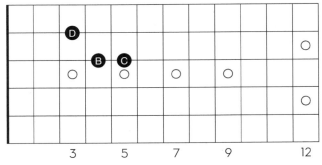

Horizontal neck grid showing 3rd position "D-B-C"

The final shift involves diagonally moving the 3rd-fret D to its unison counterpart on the 3rd string, at the 7th fret, thus completing the shift of Note Group 1 to a lower adjacent string. Just keep in mind that when shifting from the 2nd string to the 3rd string, your G–B string awareness—the fact that those strings are separated by a major 3rd as opposed to a perfect 4th, like the other string pairs—needs to be intact.

From there the process continues until you run out of either frets or strings—whichever comes first! Below you can see all of the possible neck locations for the B–C–D three-notes-per-string sequences of the same pitch.

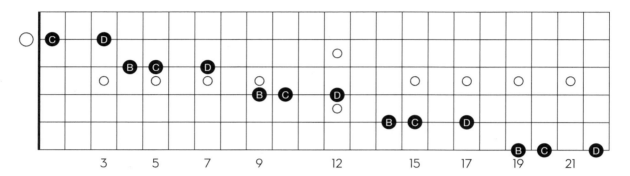

Horizontal neck grid showing locations of "B-C-D"

Not only will unison position shifts help combat the inevitable confusion guitarists encounter when reading, but they work in perfect harmony with this book's "reading recycling" methodology. So, on that note, let's go back and recycle all the B–C–D passages in this chapter with diagonally moving unison position shifts. Similarly, you should put this same process to work throughout the rest of the book.

Besides creating even more ways for you to read your Note Groups, these diagonal movements and unison position shifts help to empower your neck vision, and that makes you *a more confident reader.*

CHAPTER 4

Expanding Movements

Although the staff has five lines and four spaces, that's not enough to illustrate the pitch range of any instrument—including the guitar. To accommodate the guitar's range outside those five lines and four spaces, the staff "comes alive" via what I call *expanding movements*.

We'll begin our exploration of these expanding movements with Note Group 2, which contains what I call the "borderline" spaces of the staff. Then, we'll check out Note Group 3, which jumps off the staff completely using what you'll soon come to know as an everyday notational attribute.

Note Group 2: E–F–G

This next set of notes picks up right where Note Group 1 left off. Note Group 2 introduces the next three notes on the staff: E, F, and G.

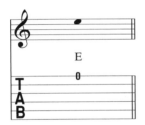

Note E with Tab

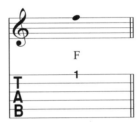

Note F with Tab

Note G with Tab

Now let's look at them all together on the staff.

Just as in Note Group 1, there's a stepwise pattern on the staff as the notes flow from E to G, this time space-line-space. The note E occupies the fourth space followed by F on the fifth line, with G sitting atop the staff in what would be the next space. This G is the first example of the staff's *expanding movements* with a note outside the basic five lines and four spaces. This "borderline" space also exists on the bottom of the staff, as you'll learn in Chapter 8.

In the neck grid below, you can see how E, F, and G in this pitch range spread across the neck through diagonal movements and unison position shifts.

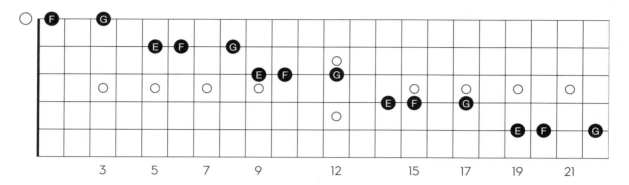

Horizontal neck grid showing locations of "E-F-G"

If you have a 24-fret neck, you can squeeze in another E on the 6th string, at the 24th fret!

Now let's combine Note Groups 1 and 2 on the staff. Notice that all six notes connect alphabetically, flowing in a sequence of alternating lines and spaces.

We will continue to "build out" your note recognition in this manner throughout the book, but first, it's time to read some E–F–G passages.

Play the following passages on the high E string in open position, using all downstrokes, with your metronome set to a comfortable tempo between 50–65 bpm, as indicated above the first example. If necessary, read one line at a time, stopping at each thin double bar line. As you recycle the passages be sure to take a breather between each pass and try to read by relationship and not just notes. See and seize the space-to-line relationship and focus on reading in chunks as opposed to one note at a time. Soon, as it comes together, you'll find yourself naturally reading ahead, and when that happens, you're on your way. And don't forget about the three reading mantras you learned in Chapter 2!

- **Always read with a metronome.**

- **Always read ahead.**

- **Don't stop.**

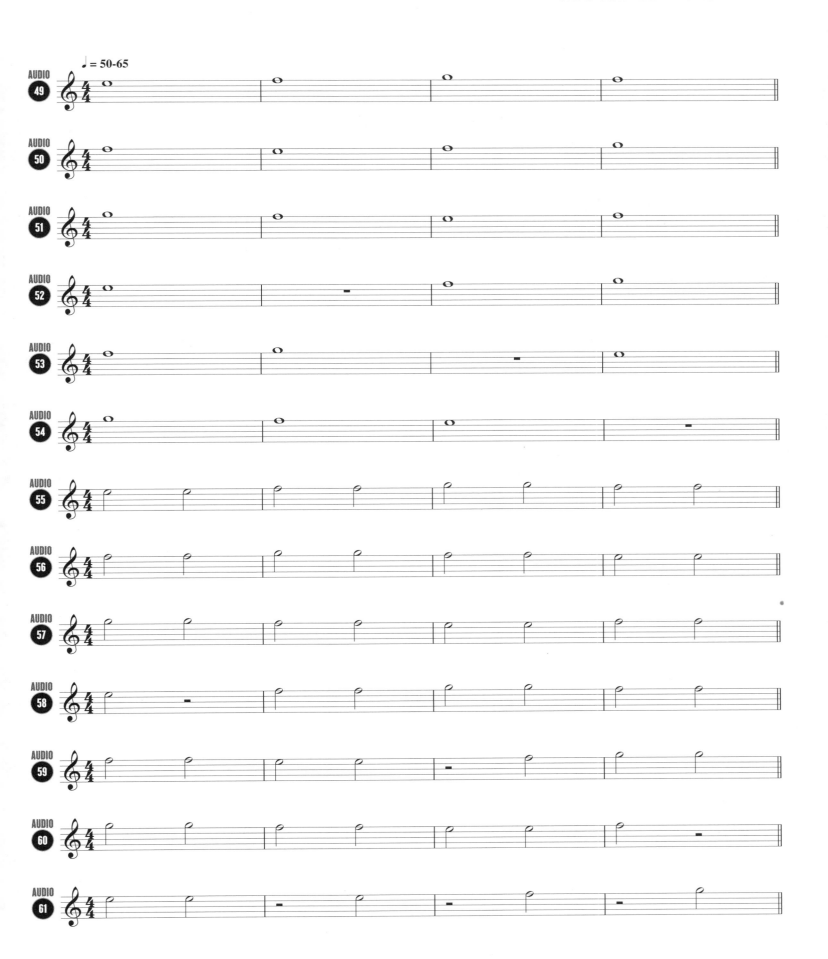

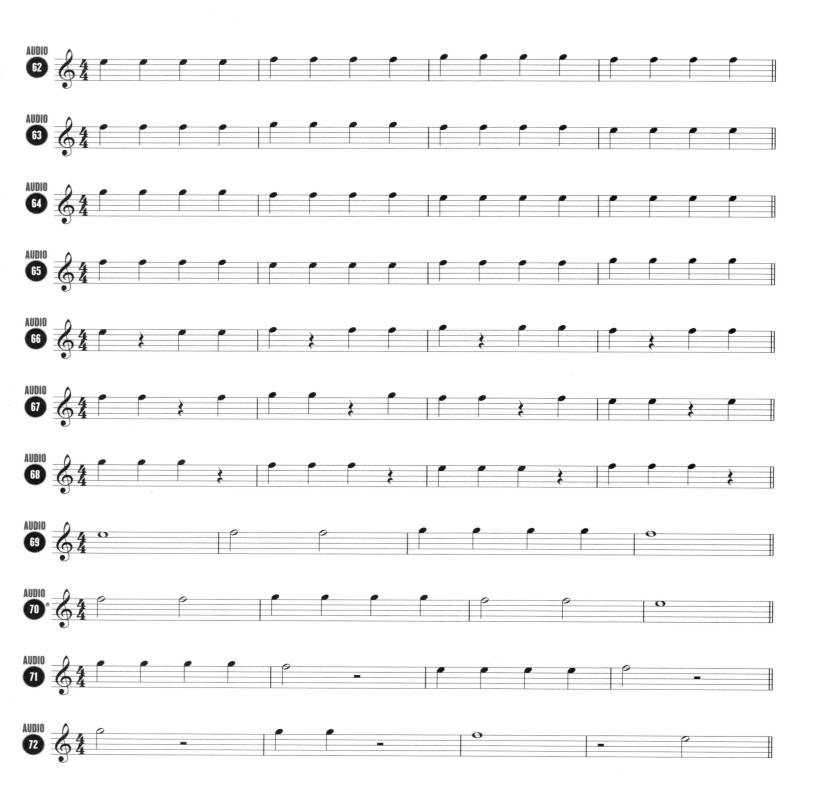

Be sure to exhaust every recycling possibility and to dedicate some time to writing your own E–F–G passages. The more time you put in, the more you'll begin to feel at ease with reading, and that, along with strong neck vision, breeds confidence.

Ledger Lines

In Chapter 1 you learned about the staff and its five-line/four-space makeup. Working with Note Group 2 you discovered there's a "borderline" space above (and below) the staff that extends its range. But your guitar can produce notes well above and below these boundaries. To depict these expanding movements, we use a notation attribute known as *ledger lines*. Ledger lines provide both lines and spaces for notes that fall outside the pitch range of the standard staff. For instance, the next note above the G that you just learned in Note Group 2 is an A. Using the alternating line-space arrangement, that A needs to sit on a line, so we simply add one above the staff, like so:

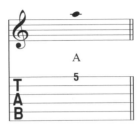

Note A with Tab

Notice that the distance from the staff's top line and the ledger line above it is the same as the four spaces within it. No matter how many ledger lines are used (above or below the staff), that spacing must be maintained. That consistency allows you to read notes not just as separate entities, but also in the logically relative fashion you learned while reading Note Groups 1–2. It's also what helps you start to read ahead in chunks, thus paving the way for you to eventually sight-read!

Note Group 3: A–B–C

To begin working with ledger lines, Note Group 3 dives right in with the A note you just learned plus the B and C notes above it.

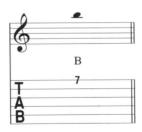

Note B with Tab

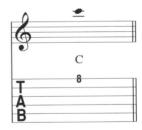

Note C with Tab

Looking at this sequence of A–B–C horizontally on the staff you can clearly see the line-to-space-to-line relationship of the ledger lines is as clear as it is when the notes fall on the standard staff, as within Note Group 1.

Note Group 3 sticks with the same melodic sequencing established in the first two Note Groups, which will provide a small yet significant mental advantage as you read and recycle the following passages. As a result, you may feel comfortable enough to start reading passages all the way to their respective terminal bar lines. Reading by relationship will help this along, but it's OK to continue reading line by line, too. Do what's best for you and your development.

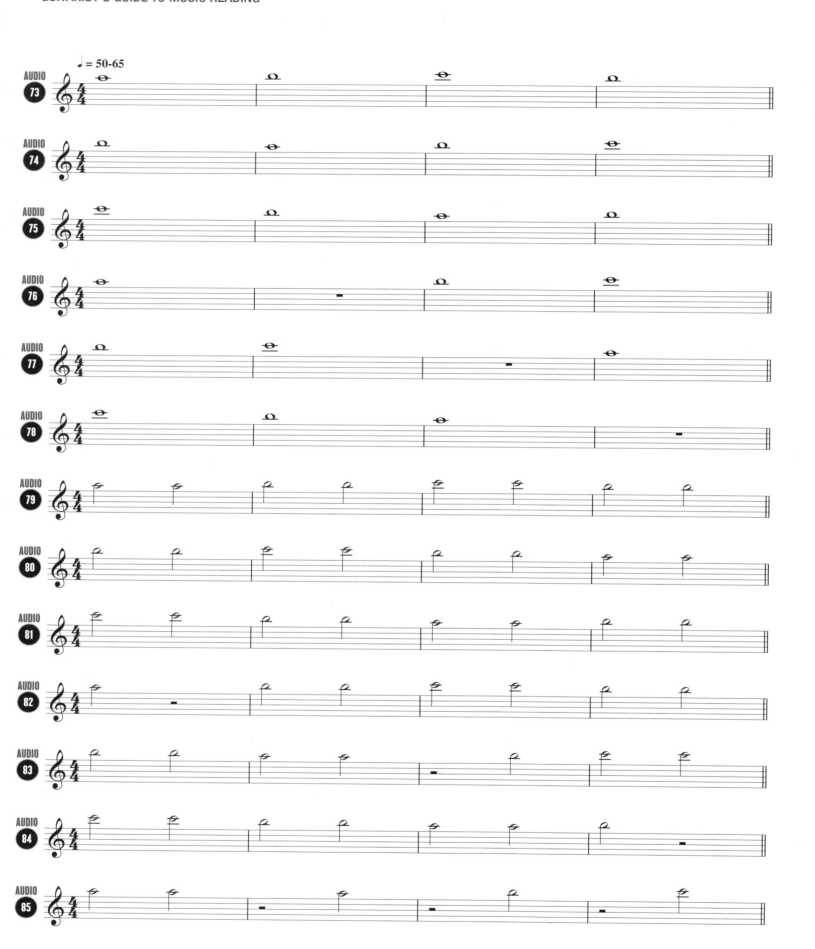

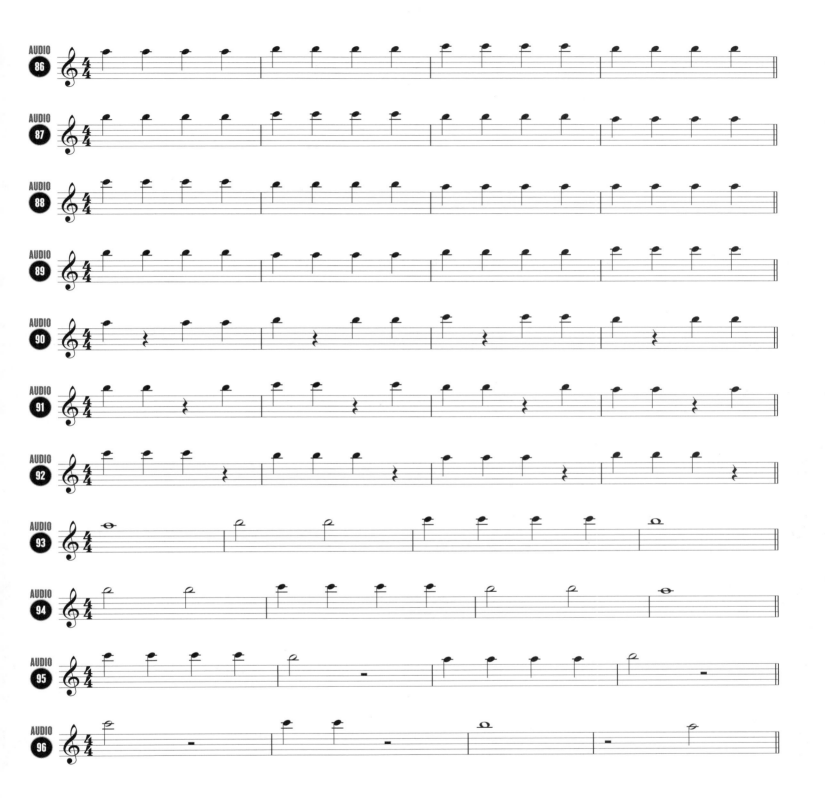

CHAPTER 5

Establishing Rhythm Recognition Skills | Subdivisions

Taking a break from the pitch element of reading music, we're going back to an *attack first, sustain later* approach via "tapping out" passages. Once again, no guitar is needed here, as you'll be tapping the rhythms you're reading with your hands against whatever you choose. When this rhythm-only reading approach was first introduced in Chapter 2, the idea was to focus on one part of the rhythm equation—the attack—as you got a handle on recognizing and tapping out downbeats. That idea continues here as you're introduced to the spaces in time that occur in between the downbeat pulse!

Subdivisions and Related Rests

By now you should be solid with this concept: A downbeat is an attack that's made in sync with the beat you're playing to. So far, that's all you've read and played, but in this chapter you'll explore the concept of *subdivisions* where note durations are less than one beat in duration and are played not only on the beat but also in between it.

Before we get into it, let's once more review the note duration hierarchy when a "4" is on the bottom of a time signature (e.g., 4/4), which indicates that the quarter note is the beat unit and holds the value of one beat:

Whole note = 4 beats

Half note = 2 beats

Quarter note = 1 beat

Eighth note = 1/2 beat

Sixteenth note = 1/4 beat

Since we're talking subdivisions, the focus here is on the last two note types—eighth and sixteenth notes and their respective rests.

Eighth note   **Eighth rest**   **Sixteenth note**   **Sixteenth rest**

The eighth note splits a quarter note, or the beat, into two equal parts, whereas the sixteenth note chops it up into four equal parts. (What about *three* equal parts, you ask? Those are called *triplets*, and you'll learn about those in Chapter 11.) The following two sections will explain the ins and outs of recognizing and interpreting each subdivision, and then throw you right into the fire with some reading passages so you can develop your rhythm recognition skills as you tap them out.

Eighth Notes

Eighth notes are the most basic—and common—subdivisions, as they split the beat evenly in half. You're already familiar with the first half—the downbeat. The other half, aptly called the *upbeat*, is attacked exactly in the middle of two pulses. Given this reference to two pulses, it's important to realize this is not to say two eighth notes last more than the duration of one complete beat, it's just the following downbeat serves as a definite indicator as to when the upbeat has rang out for the correct duration. This will come in handy when you start playing upbeat eighth notes later in the book.

Flags and Beams

As you probably noticed at the start of this chapter, a single eighth note has a *flag* affixed to its stem. This is how you'll see it notated when eighth notes are singled out by rests, as seen here.

When eighth notes are strung together in consecutive downbeat and upbeat rhythms, a *beam* is used to link a series of two or more of them. Note that the measure is divided evenly in half as well; that is, the beam does not cross over from the upbeat of beat 2 to the downbeat of beat 3—and it never will. This is just a standard sheet music convention, to help make reading easier.

Tapping & Counting Out With Eighth Note Subdivisions

You first started to develop your rhythm recognition skills in Chapter 2, via the exercise of tapping out passages. If you'll recall, one of the approaches you were asked to apply was to count out the meter, counting downbeats only. Now we're going to augment that approach and count out the subdivisions at the same time.

Learning the "feel" of eighth notes is much easier when they're in a consecutive series of beamed downbeats and upbeats, so that's where we'll begin—but you're also going to count out the meter. Since these passages are in 4/4, your downbeat count remains "1-2-3-4," but now you'll call out the upbeats as well, saying "and" between the downbeat numbers, like this:

1   and   2   and   3   and   4   and

With your metronome set at a tempo within the indicated range of 50–65 bpm, that's comfortable enough for you to look ahead, tap out the following four-bar passages while counting out the downbeats and upbeats. When you come upon the quarter rests, continue to count both the downbeat and the upbeats. By the way, if you happen to notice any patterns, you're not imagining things. But more on that later.

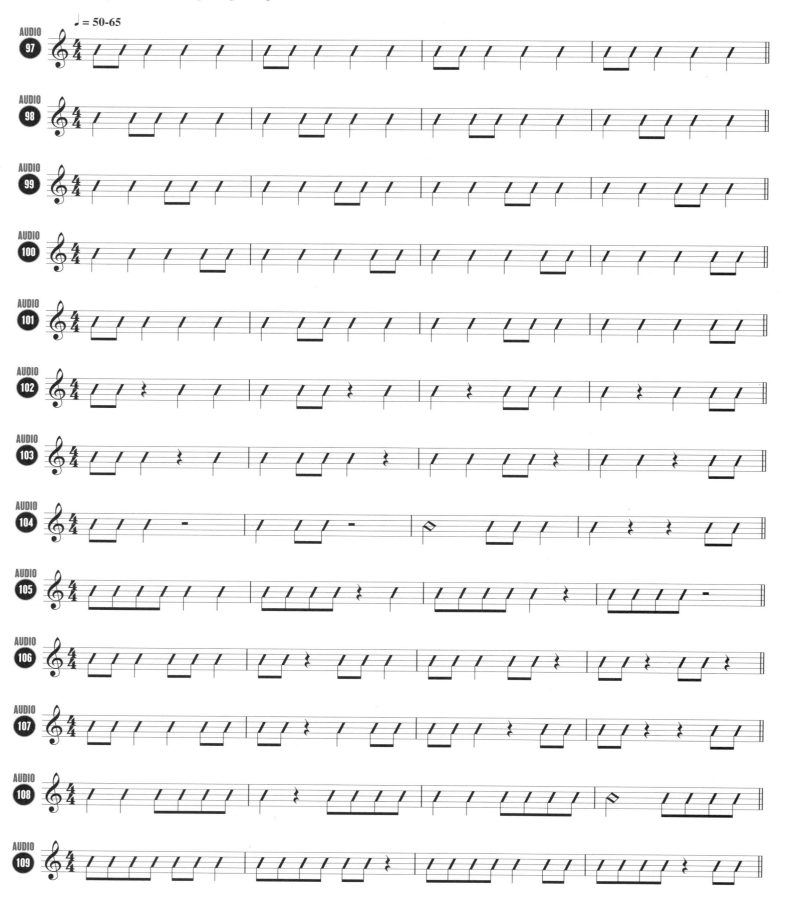

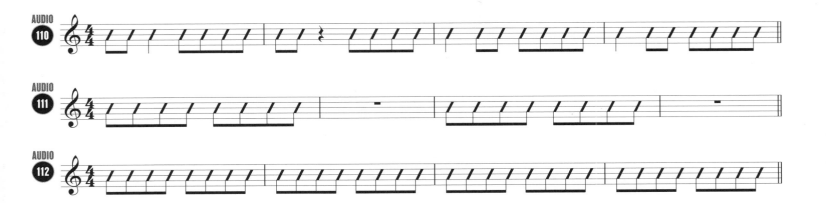

THE POWER OF THE FOOT

When I first tackled eighth notes, I found it hard to nail the upbeats accurately—especially at slower tempos. And because the goal here is to build your rhythm recognition skills, speeding up the tempo is not an option, since you'll inevitably lose sight of what you're reading. So to stay on track with the right approach and read with a manageable tempo, I paid close attention to an unlikely ally—my foot. I often tap my foot when playing, and I trained myself to tap my foot so that I was lifting my foot *precisely in the middle* of two downbeats surrounding it—aka the upbeat. Doing this helped to steer the focus on the feel away from my hands, which were already busy tapping and later *playing*. If you had trouble with these first passages, try tapping your foot to keep the pulse; it may just do the trick—did for me!

Sixteenth Notes

Sixteenth notes are the next level of subdivisions in the "multiples of two" hierarchy, splitting the beat into *four* equal parts. Since you're now familiar with eighth note subdivisions and their two-part downbeat/upbeat architecture, you can think of sixteenth notes as dividing the duration of each eighth note in half—or, splitting your split!

Flags and Beams

Whereas a single eighth note has a flag, single sixteenth notes have *two* flags attached to their stems. Likewise, sixteenth rests also have an added "flag."

Just like eighth notes, consecutive sixteenth notes make use of beams, only they're doubled, as shown here.

Tapping & Counting Out With Sixteenth Note Subdivisions

Going back to the "split your split" concept, a full beat's worth of sixteenth notes involve four components, two of which you already know—the downbeat and upbeat. You'll still count the meter out (1-2-3-4) to mark the downbeat and you'll still count the upbeat as "and." But here's where the next split comes in: Between those two shout-outs are the *off-beats*. To count these, the second and fourth sixteenth notes, you use the syllabic elements "ee" and "uh." Sound hard? Nah, just look at it here.

Once again, with your metronome set at a tempo within the indicated range of 50–65 bpm, that's comfortable enough for you to start looking ahead, tap out the following four-bar passages while counting out all four sixteenth notes. Remember, it may be easier to keep the sixteenth-note count going even when you're on a quarter rest. If you notice any patterns, welcome them with open arms—that element eventually will become your best friend, especially when reading down chord charts.

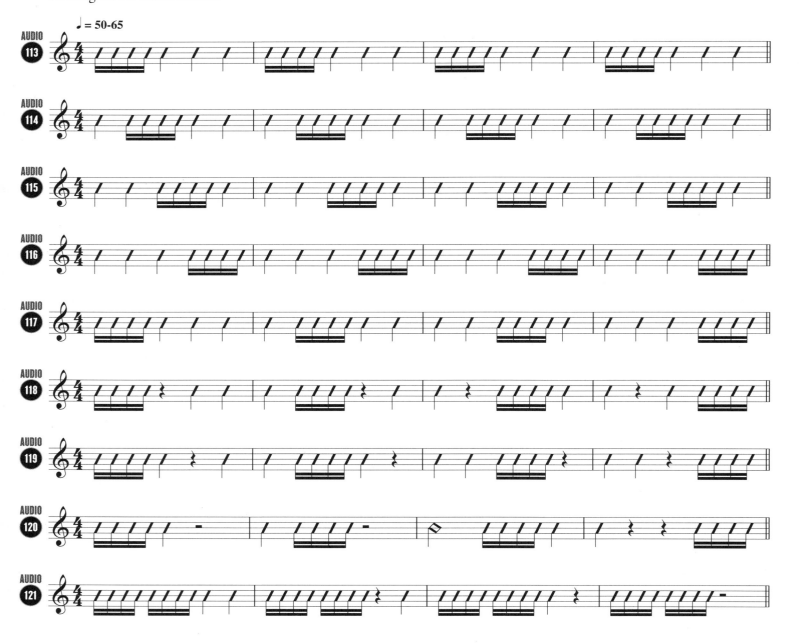

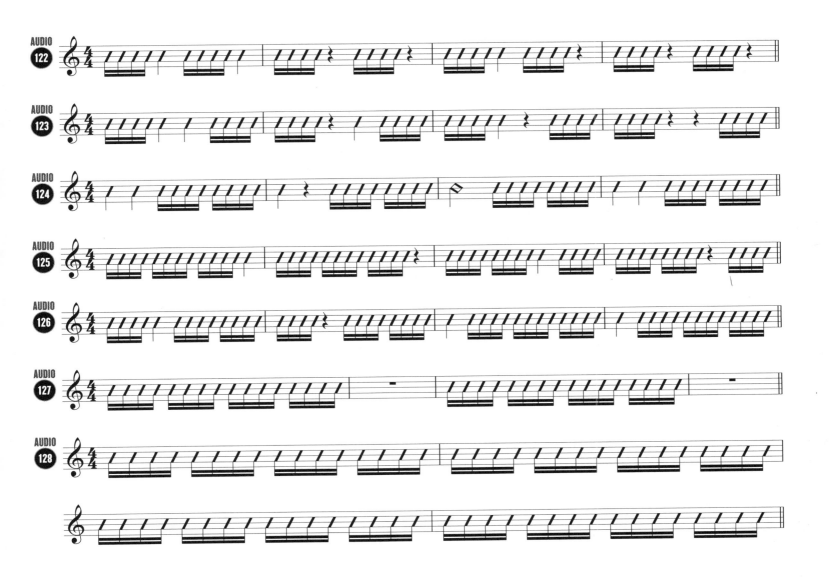

OK, time to recycle those passages for added practice. Then create a few of your own. Because these are solely rhythm-based with the pitch element out of the picture, they should come rather quickly.

RECYCLED COUNTING

To add to the many recycling approaches you've already learned, here's one that may seem simple, but is actually a very beneficial challenge. Go back and again tap out all the eighth- and sixteenth-note passages presented in this chapter, but this time count the meter using *only* downbeats (1-2-3-4), while tapping the written rhythms. Sounds easy enough, but you'll see that keeping a downbeat-only count is tricky because you have more coming at you than just that with all the subdivisions. This is the level you want your counting feel to reach, because it requires a strong rhythmic foundation that can't be swayed by rhythmic variances. In the end, that foundation makes you a better reader since you can focus on the music overall rather than sweating all the details.

Syncopated Subdivision Tapping and Counting

Having recycled the previous sections of rhythmic passages, you should now have the beginnings of a solid feel for—as well as eye for—recognizing eighth- and sixteenth-note subdivisions and how to count them. This next section shifts from the array of consecutively beamed subdivisions you've read thus far and replaces them with more complex rhythms that seem to place attacks in irregular and unexpected parts of the beat, aka *syncopation*. We'll steer you into the world of syncopated rhythms gradually, but get used to them, as they are what makes music move and groove.

Syncopated Eighths and Quarter Notes

When you first started to tap out rhythms, you had the advantage of knowing that something always happened on a downbeat. Now we're going to raise the ante and make you pay attention to what is happening on both the downbeat and upbeat at all times. The trick with effectively reading under these conditions, as well as with more difficult syncopated rhythms, is one you already know—look ahead!

To kick off your syncopated rhythm recognition quest, we've got a collection of passages that emphasize upbeat eighth notes as well as upbeat *quarter notes*. It's even more important now that you set your metronome at a tempo between 50–65 bpm that allows you to comfortably read ahead. Carefully tap out the rhythms and heed this hint wisely: Look for two- and four-beat patterns.

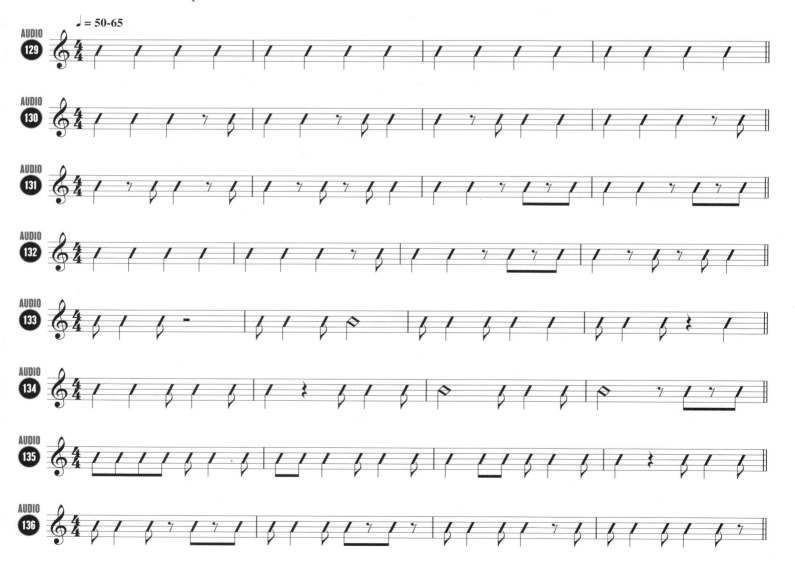

Offbeat Sixteenths

Syncopated sixteenths are some of my favorite rhythms to read. They're uniquely challenging and sound incredible when played precisely. As you read through these next passages, you'll find them becoming more and more "broken up." Just as you did in the syncopated eighths passages, look for recurring patterns. With syncopated sixteenths, it could be as small as one beat. Whatever the case, the more you can recognize these chunks of rhythm, the easier it is to continually read ahead, and once that's in place, there's no stoppin' you.

Continuing to count all subdivisions out loud, set your metronome to a tempo between 50–65 bpm. If at any time you feel you need to go below 50 bpm here, do it. Sixteenths are more forgiving at slow tempos since there are more of them in between the beats.

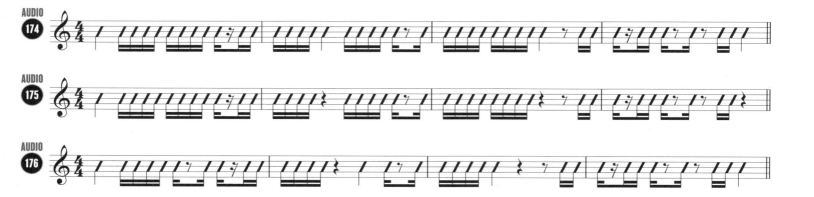

Common Rhythmic Motives

In music there exists the term *motive*, or *motif*, which is used to describe short, recurring, tangible ideas that can be rhythmic and/or melodic. Remember how I kept dropping hints to look for patterns in the earlier reading passages? Those were motives.

In the passages you've read so far in this chapter, you encountered many common rhythmic motives that you're sure to see again and again. Below is a list of the motives. Study them, befriend them, and learn them well—you've not seen the last of them.

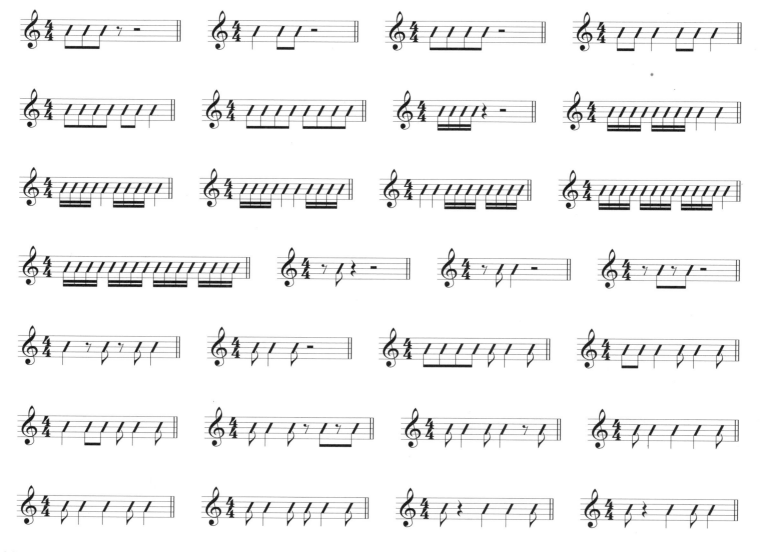

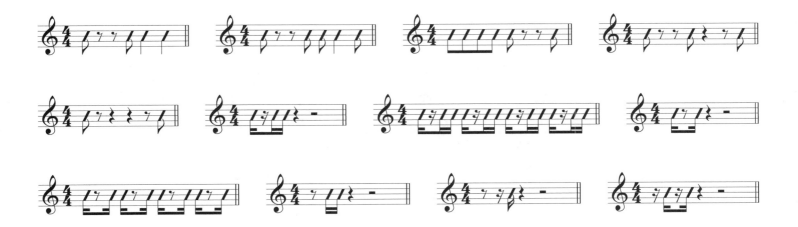

Motives play a vital role in reading ahead. When developing this skill, you eventually want to look more than just a note or two ahead; you want—make that *need*—to see at least two beats, and eventually full bars, ahead. One way to do that is to look for these one- and two-beat motives. Then, when you combine rhythmic awareness with melodic-based motives, such as arpeggio sequences or melodies that move in scale steps, you'll start to see sheet music in a whole different way.

On that note, when composing your own practice passages, start to write in motives. Even though your goal is utilitarian, you may find your artistic melodic writing begin to take shape as an added bonus.

CHAPTER 6

Visualization and the Power of the Octave

Now that you have you logged some time reading and tapping rhythm subdivisions, let's bring back the pitch element. Using the three Note Groups you've already learned, we're now going to show you a visualization technique that applies both to the neck and the sheet music, where you organize your neck into *one-octave cells*. This will help you choose where on the neck to position your hand and provide a reliable backdrop when making position shifts. To take full advantage of one-octave cells as well as a concept called *octave shifting*, I'll hip you to an underlying pattern of note locations, based on octaves, that you can use to move up and down the neck when position shifts are required.

Note Group 4: One-Octave C Major Scale

If you combine the three Note Groups studied thus far, you'll find that they form a one-octave C major scale, with an added 7th degree (B) as the lowest note. This composite forms Note Group 4, which you'll begin using in 5th position, as shown below.

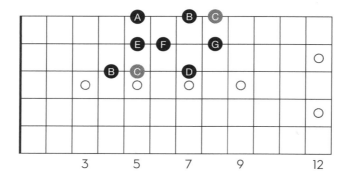

Even though you're reading in a new position, the note locations on the staff are the same as what you already know. As you read through the following charts, set your metronome at a comfortable tempo within the indicated range of 50–65 bpm and keep your fret hand's first finger anchored on the 5th fret. From there the fingerings will fall naturally into place. As for the 4th-fret B on the 3rd string, simply lower your first finger one fret (half step) when the middle-line B needs to be played. Remember to look for patterns in both rhythm and melody and use the line-space relationship to your advantage. If you see a succession of line-to-space or space-to-line sequences, the melody is moving in scale steps.

Before you tackle the practice passages, it's a good idea for you to play this C major scale on its own, to a click playing quarter-, eighth-, and sixteenth-note rhythms, to familiarize yourself with the pitch and rhythm recognition components throughout.

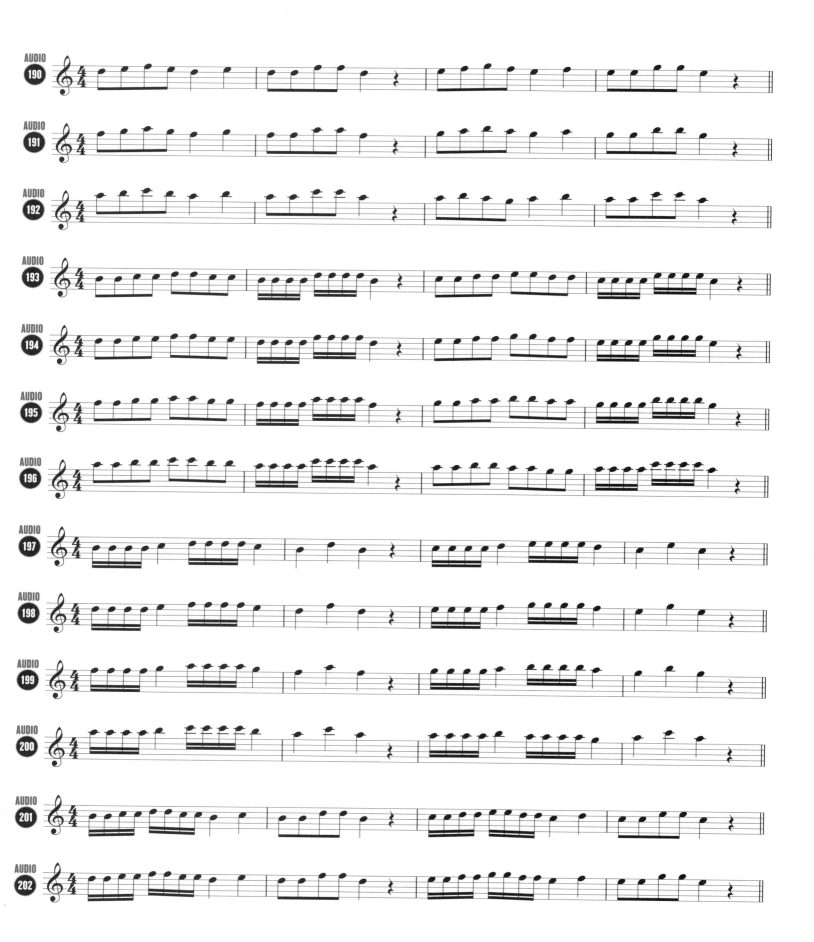

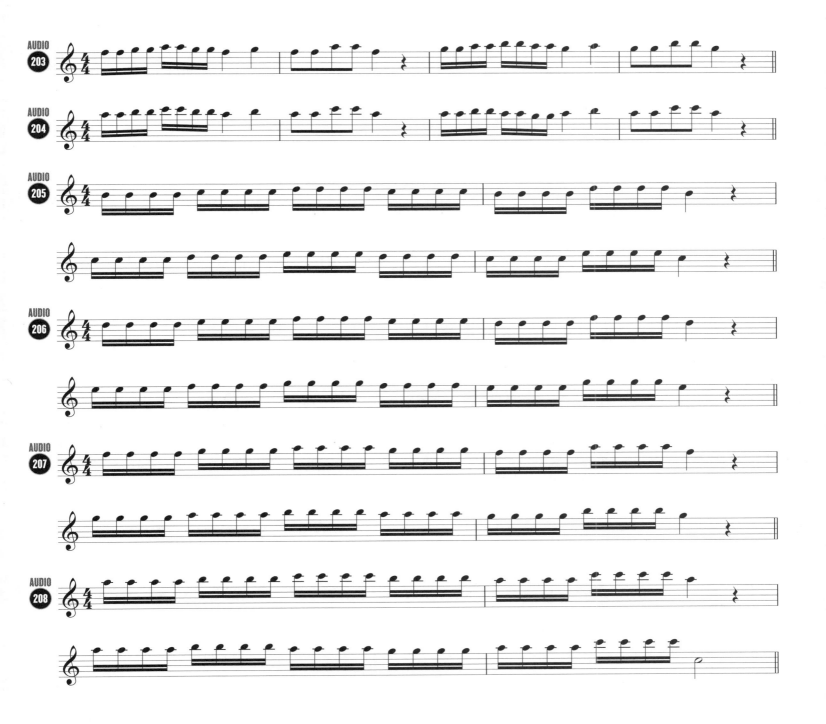

Of all the recycling methods introduced so far, the most pertinent in regards to one-octave cells are unison position shifts by way of diagonally shifting the cell to the next lower adjacent string set, like this:

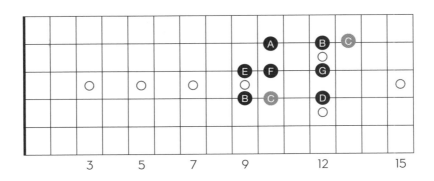

Although the one-octave cell retains the same exact notes, you can see that the relative locations of three-note-per-string sequences have changed. This time, the two lower sequences both line up on the 9th fret instead of being off by a half step (one fret) as in the previous position. If your G–B string awareness is tingling, your intuition serves you well. Because the E–F–G sequence was fretted on the B string in the first version of the cell, in 5th position, it must be lowered a half step when diagonally shifted to the lower, adjacent G string, in 9th position. This happens again when the entire cell shifts to the next lower adjacent string set, in 14th position, at which point all *three* sequences line up at the 14th fret.

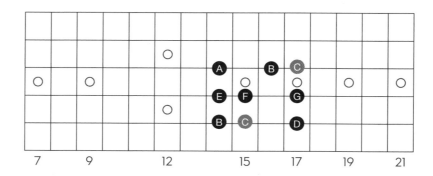

Now go back and re-read the chart in these two new positions and don't forget to apply all the other recycling methods. As you do so, you're not only building your one-octave cell and shifting vision but also further exercising your pitch/rhythm recognition skills, with the bonus of flexing your reading-ahead skills. When you've exhausted this chapter's passages, put the time into strategically composing your own. Remember, the key is *slight* variation. It allows you to read with stress-free familiarity with the simultaneous beneficial challenge of variation.

AVAILABLE POSITIONS

Whenever you see the term "position," it's referring to the fret location on the neck where your fret hand's index finger is anchored. From there the remaining fingers fall chromatically into place up the neck; that is, in "5th position," your index finger plays the notes on the 5th fret, your middle finger the notes on the 6th fret, your ring finger the notes on the 7th fret, and your pinky the notes on the 8th fret. In classical and occasionally other forms of sheet music, the position is indicated with a Roman numeral, like "Position V," for 5th position.

Recall that the first one-octave cell was called out as being in 5th position, but there was a note on the 4th fret of the G string. Though that note is played with your first finger, your hand should be "positioned" on the 5th fret since the cell centers itself there. Thus positions also should include the possibility of the first finger occasionally dropping down a half step from the central point as well as the fourth (pinky) finger occasionally moving *up* a half step.

Being able to recognize and reap the benefits of positions when available helps your reading become more consistent, thus making you more confident.

Octave Climbing

Many melodies, especially simple ones, can be played in a single position and feel like the one-octave cell seen in Note Group 4. Of course, there are myriad position and cell approaches, and as you read and study a guitar's neck geometry, you'll start to formulate your own preferred visions. Whatever those may be, being able to shift positions and/or cells is an important skill to develop.

One way to make your move is to use octaves as your guide. Octaves can be played up and down the neck in a consistent, albeit slightly jagged, pattern. Check out the C octave pattern starting on the 1st fret of the B string that progresses all the way up to a 22nd-fret C on the D string.

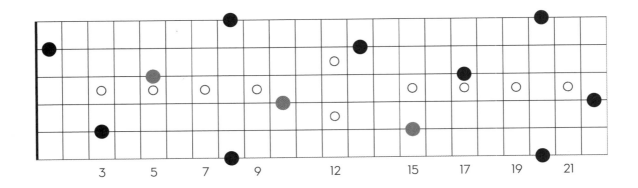

Note the C notes in grey; those were the roots of the three one-octave cells introduced earlier in this chapter. If you were unsure of how those one-octave cells were relocated, understanding these octave locations will help you see it more clearly (and don't forget your G–B string awareness). You should also be aware that not every point in the framework will work as an axis for all devices; for example, you wouldn't be able to play the current build of the one-octave cell off any 2nd- or 1st-string C notes. You can still use this knowledge, however, to play simpler sequences made of up three notes, similar to the first ones you learned.

To more easily see the pattern, we must first establish a way to recognize the various steps in the climb. A great way to do that is through the commonly used chord vision method known as the CAGED system, where the five basic open chords are linked together in a consistent sequence across the neck. Here you see how the C octaves exist within those chord shape callouts.

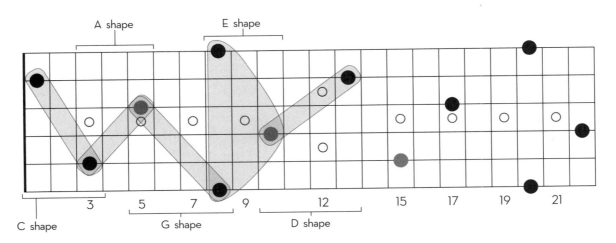

Going up the neck past the D shape, the CAGED system recycles itself in the same order all the way up to the E shape (20th fret) before running out real estate. Once you have this connection system memorized, it's just a matter of knowing where each key begins. Don't worry—I did the work for you! Here are the Octave Frames for all 12 keys. Play through them all (don't forget the open strings, where available), naming the CAGED system chord shape associated with each octave pair, for added reinforcement.

C Octave Frame

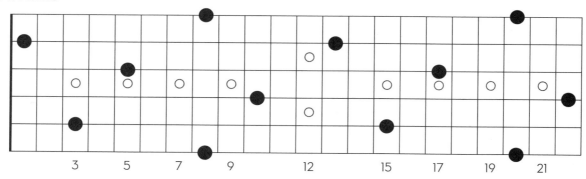

C♯/D♭ Octave Frame

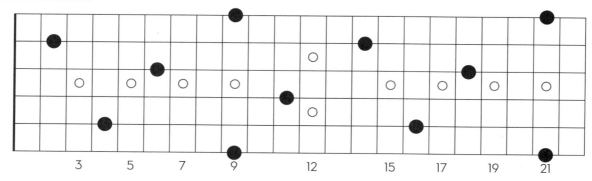

D Octave Frame

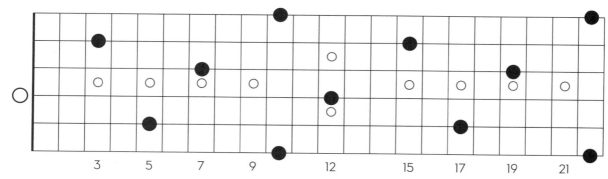

D♯/E♭ Octave Frame

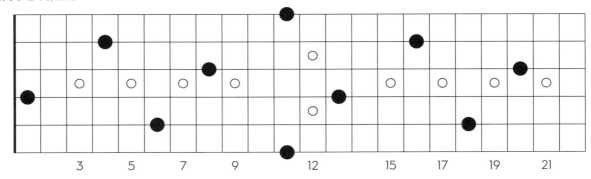

E Octave Frame

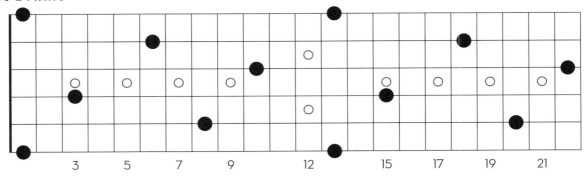

E♯/F Octave Frame

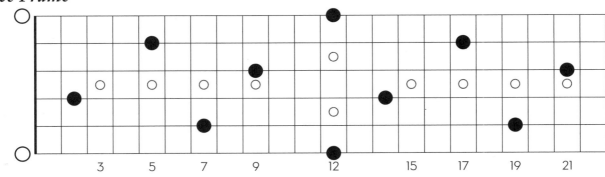

F♯/G♭ Octave Frame

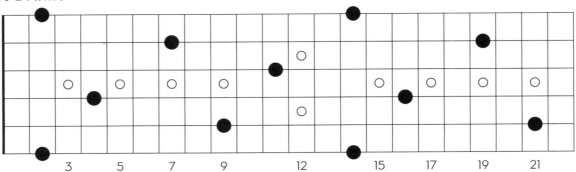

G Octave Frame

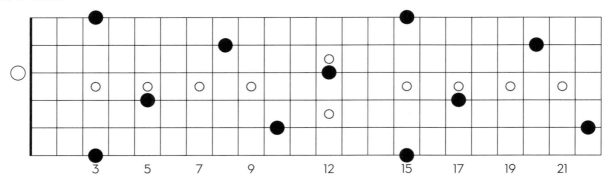

G#/A♭ Octave Frame

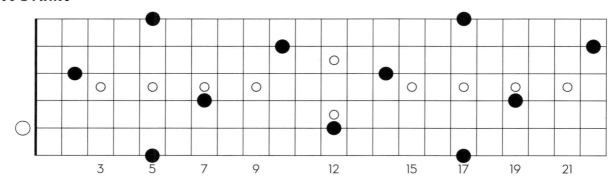

A Octave Frame

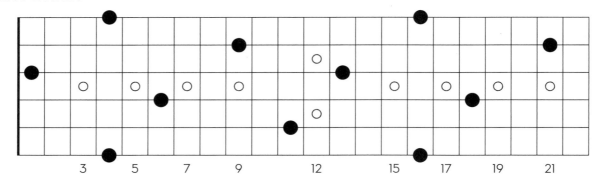

A#/B♭ Octave Frame

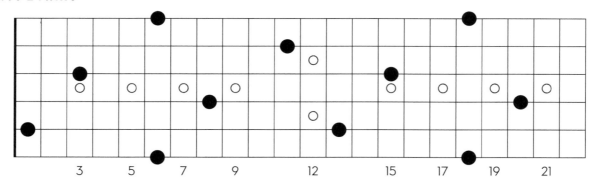

B Octave Frame

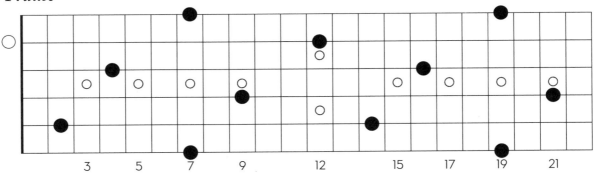

Octave Shifts

Through diagonal movements and unison position shifting, you earlier learned how to move the location of a Note Group to other strings while remaining in the same pitch range. For example, Note Group 1 (B–C–D) was introduced in open position:

But it can also be played at these locations:

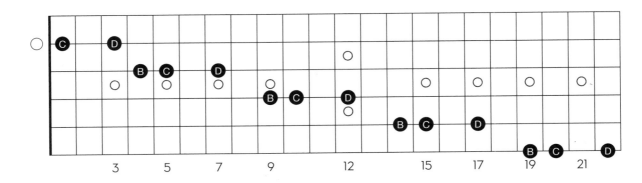

Now that you're getting your head (and hands) around the octave patterns across the entire neck, try shifting and playing the Note Groups in higher and lower octave ranges. For instance, try reading the Note Group 1 chart (page 11) in these locations:

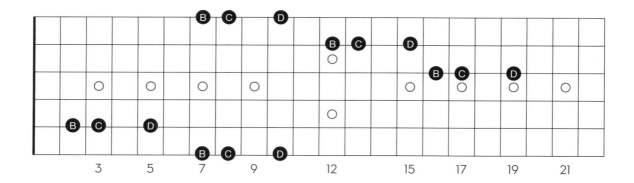

Be aware that this is not just an exercise in reading. Shifting melodies in octaves on the fly is entry-level transposing—a skill you'll be expected to have as a reading, professional guitarist. As a matter of fact, you've been octave shifting from the first note you read in this book. Check it out: Guitar notation instructs us to read an octave *lower* than concert pitch dictates. That is, if a piano player were to play a guitar melody "as written," it would properly sound an octave higher than when played on the guitar. The reason for this adjustment, as with other instruments, is to accommodate the range of said instrument to the staff.

CHAPTER 7

Essential Notation Components, Part 1

At this point, you should have a solid foundation in the basic rhythm- and pitch-related concepts required to read simple melodies on your instrument. You also have a handful of ways to recycle what you're reading, providing you access to lots of fresh reading scenarios without being overwhelmed and having to resort to memorization. Furthermore, you've been gathering vital neck visualization concepts along the way that will not only help you become a good reader, but also a more confident guitarist all around.

This chapter introduces essential components used in music notation to convey various articulations. These fall under both rhythmic and pitch-related umbrellas, with rhythm leading the way. But before digging into these articulations, let's take a look at your new Note Group, which comprises a single sequence of two whole steps.

Note Group 5: G–A–B

To help accommodate the upcoming notation components, Note Group 5 steps down the staff, beginning with the G note on the second line, followed by A in the second space, and B on the third line (line-staff-line flow). The tablature indicates where you should play these three pitches.

**Note G with Tab
(5th position)**

**Note A with Tab
(5th position)**

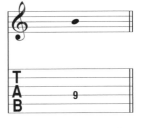

**Note B with Tab
(5th position)**

The G and A pitches presented here have yet to be seen on the staff. The B, however, is the same pitch (middle line) as the open-string B learned in Chapter 3. The reason for this shift is to address the double whole-step span of the Note Group. Below you can see the Note Group strung together in linear fashion along with my suggested fingering.

I prefer a 1–2–4 fingering approach (as opposed to 1–3–4) because of their respective independence; I find that the third finger is too interdependent on its neighboring digits. Plus, as you descend a double whole-step fingering, you'll appreciate the added reach a 1–2–4 fingering facilitates.

After you read the upcoming Note Group 5 passages in 5th position, be sure to play them in other positions on the neck using unison position shifts. In addition to ascending diagonally, don't forget to *descend* diagonally, all the way down to the open position. While it may be tempting to play that B on the open 2nd string, stay the course and keep it on the 4th fret of the G string, like this:

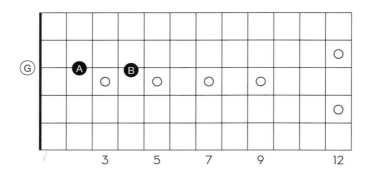

While you're at it, don't forget about the many other recycling methods introduced so far, including:

- Turning over the book and reading upside down.
- Reading the page vertically in columns.
- Reading through double bar lines to extend the four-bar passages into much longer melody streams.
- Reading across even/odd numbered pages (where possible).

And don't forget these:

- Always read with a metronome.
- Always read ahead.
- Never stop.

If you get stuck on a particular rhythm, step back and tap it out, then try again.

Read the following passages at a tempo within the range of 50–65 bpm while keeping your fret hand's 1st finger local to the 5th fret, using the suggested 1–2–4 fingering.

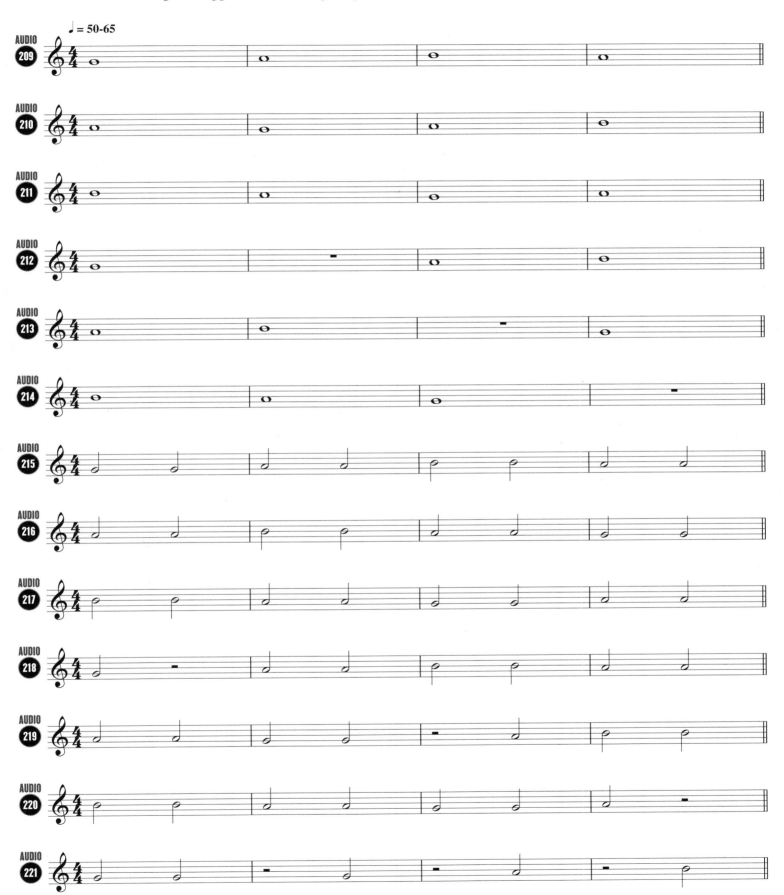

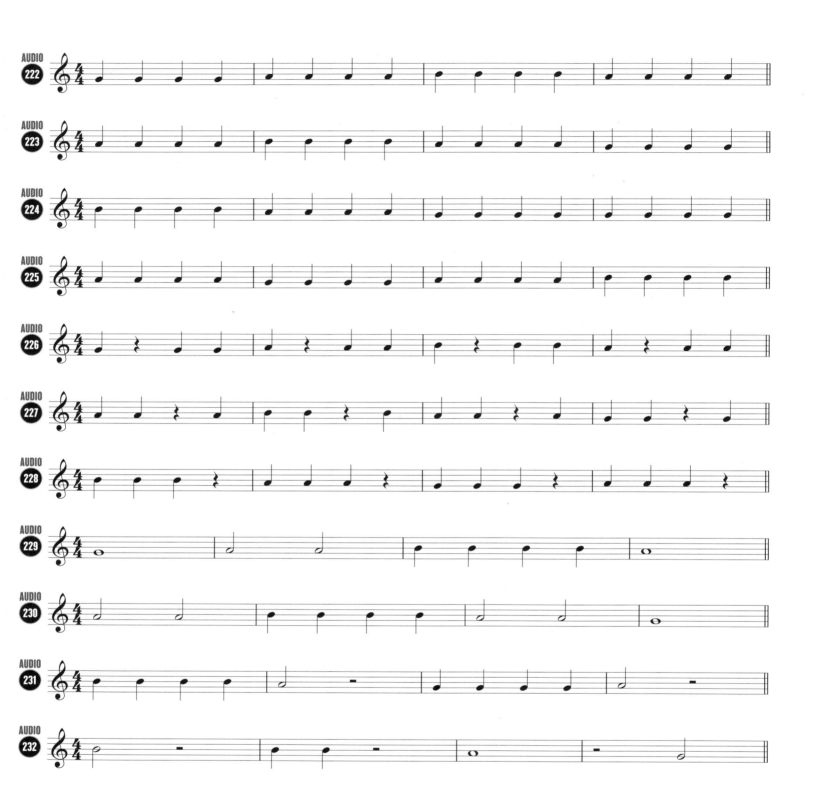

Staccato

OK, ready for those essential rhythm components? Great, let's get started. The first articulation we're going to cover is called *staccato*, which instructs the player (that's you!) to shorten a note's duration following the attack. For guitarists, it merely means relieving the downward pressure on a string against a fret, or damping an open string. The staccato articulation is indicated via a small dot either above or below the notehead.

Whether the dot is above or below depends on the direction in which the note's stem is pointing. An upstemmed note, like the G and A above, will have the staccato placed below the notehead; a downstemmed note, like the B, will have the staccato marking above the notehead. The staccato sign will always be opposite the stem.

The dynamic of your staccato playing in most instances shouldn't be so drastic that the attacked note takes on more of a percussive role than a melodic one. Listen to the accompanying CD to hear how the staccato notes should be played.

Keeping with Note Group 5, read the following passages under the same guidelines you just did. Considering you must now watch for these staccato marks, it's even more important to read ahead, so set your metronome to a tempo that allows you to do so easily.

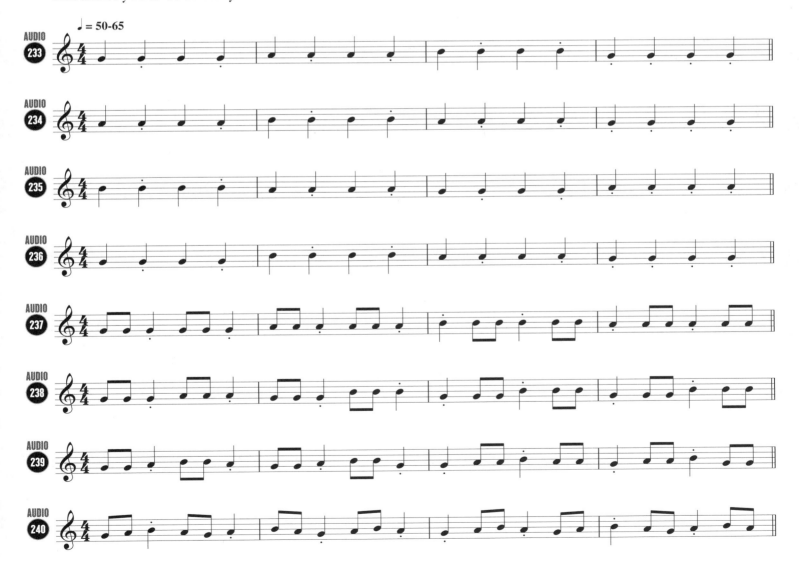

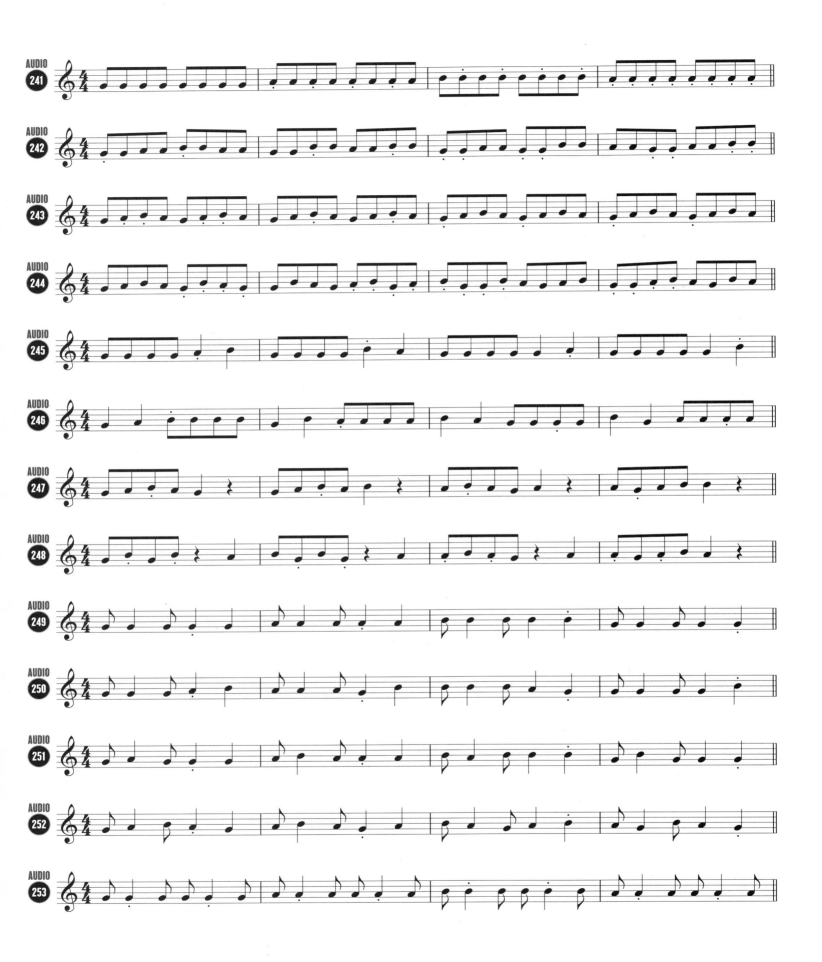

Dotted Notes

Whereas a dot above or below a notehead denotes a staccato attack, a dot placed *next to* a notehead increases that note's duration by half. For example, a dot placed next to a quarter note adds the duration of an eighth note as well, so in 4/4 time, where the quarter note is worth one beat, a dotted quarter is equal to one and a half beats.

Here are other dotted note values, assuming 4/4 time.

Dotted **half** note = **3** beats

Dotted **quarter** note = **1-1/2** beats

Dotted **eighth** note = **3/4** beat

Considering these durations, here are a couple of caveats to keep in mind:

- Whole notes may be dotted (equal to six beats), but not in 4/4 time. The meter must be at least that value (e.g., 6/4) for it to be correctly placed.

- While a sixteenth note *can* be dotted, it's incredibly rare and, depending on how fast the tempo is, it's near impossible to discern such a minute time interval. At this level of reading there's no need to explore those rhythmic possibilities.

In the following passages, you will revisit Note Group 1. Note that the B in Note Groups 1 and 5 share the same pitch. The idea here is to begin to establish recognition and reaction skills for the many instances where you'll need to make the call on a note that could be played in two different locations.

Here, assuming you're working the area of the 5th position, the B note *could* be played on the D string, at the 9th fret, as in Note Group 5. But there is a simpler alternative: Play in 4th position, with your index finger covering the B on the G string at the 4th fret, your middle finger the C (5th fret), and your pinky the D (7th fret). So set your metronome at a tempo within the indicated range of 50–65 bpm and play these passages in 4th position, reading ahead to nail those dotted notes along the way.

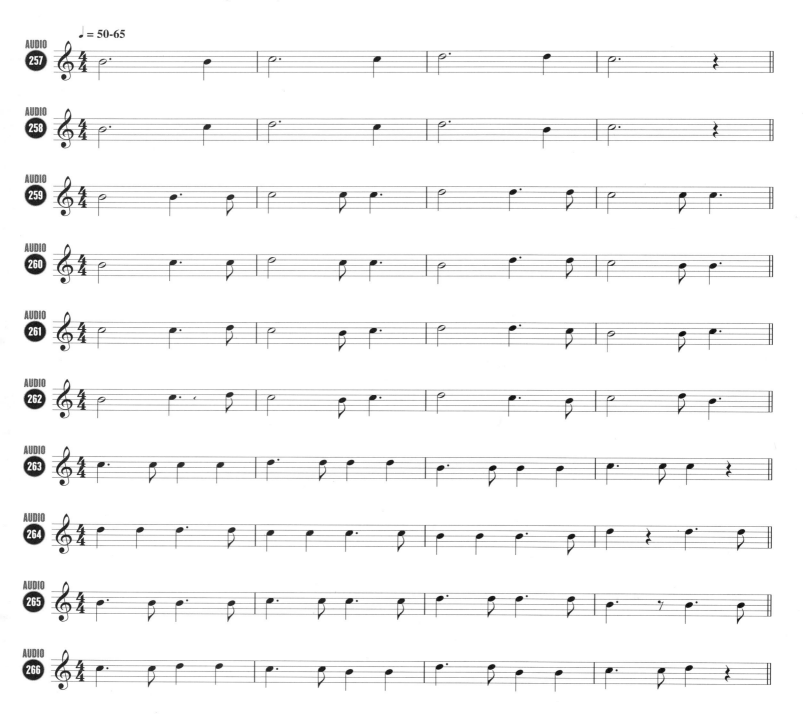

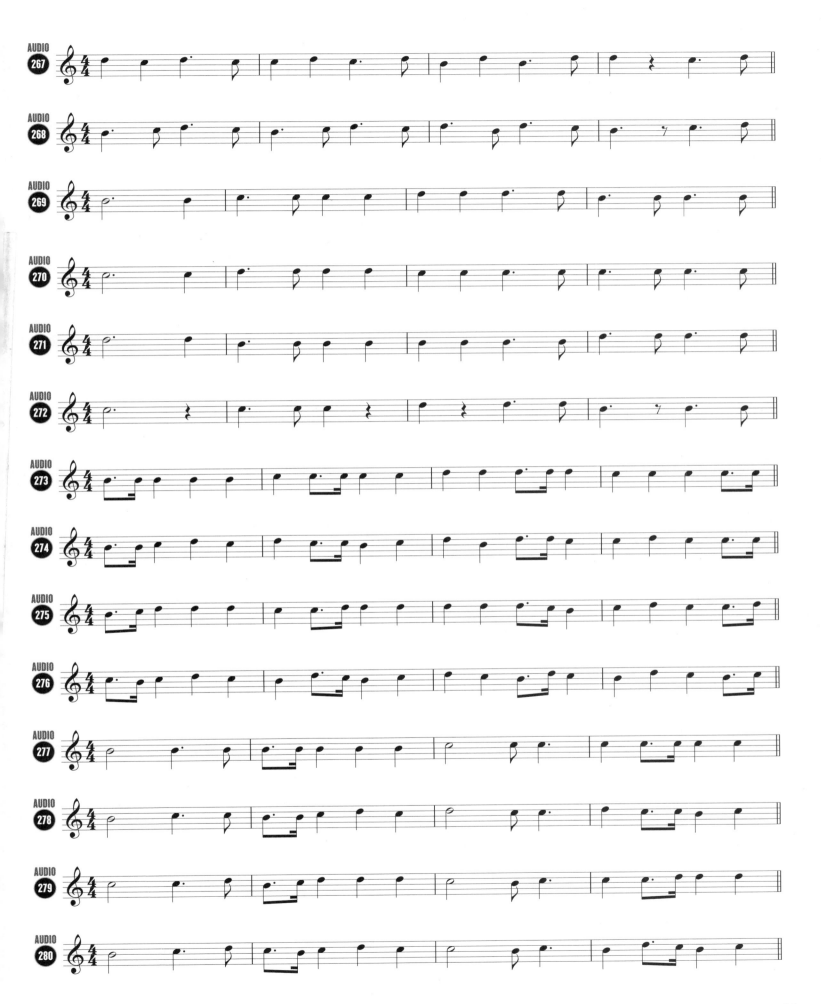

Ties

The third notation component you'll learn in this chapter is the *tie*, which essentially is a musical "plus sign." It's represented as a curved line that connects two notes *of the same pitch*, indicating they should be played as one.

Although both dots and ties increase a note's value, only the tie can extend it across bar lines.

Ties can even tie together multiple instances of the same note.

To work on reading with ties, we're going introduce a couple of new variables, but it's in the context of an old friend. For these next passages, we're going to bring back Note Group 2 (E–F–G). Originally presented in open position, we're now going to play it in 5th position, on the B string, by way of unison position shifting. We're also expanding your reading passages to eight bars, to help prepare you for what's to come at the close of this chapter.

Set your metronome at a tempo in the range of 50–65 bpm, but before you play the passages, you may want to first tap them out—even better, try doing so while counting out the rhythms.

Also, note that many of the ties presented in the following example typically are *not* found in conventional notation. For example, the very first example begins with a half note tied to a quarter note; by conventional notation rules, that would be presented simply as a dotted half note. You'll also see eighth and sixteenth notes tied in unconventional ways in this chart. I've presented it in this manner to give you plenty of practice with the "math" of reading ties. Plus, when you're on a gig in the "real world," you will frequently come across unconventional notation like this, so you should be prepared for anything!

That being said, immediately following this chart you'll find another containing the exact same melodies, but written within the rules of conventional notation. Read it in both versions (the audio is exactly the same), and you'll be ready for whatever is thrown your way.

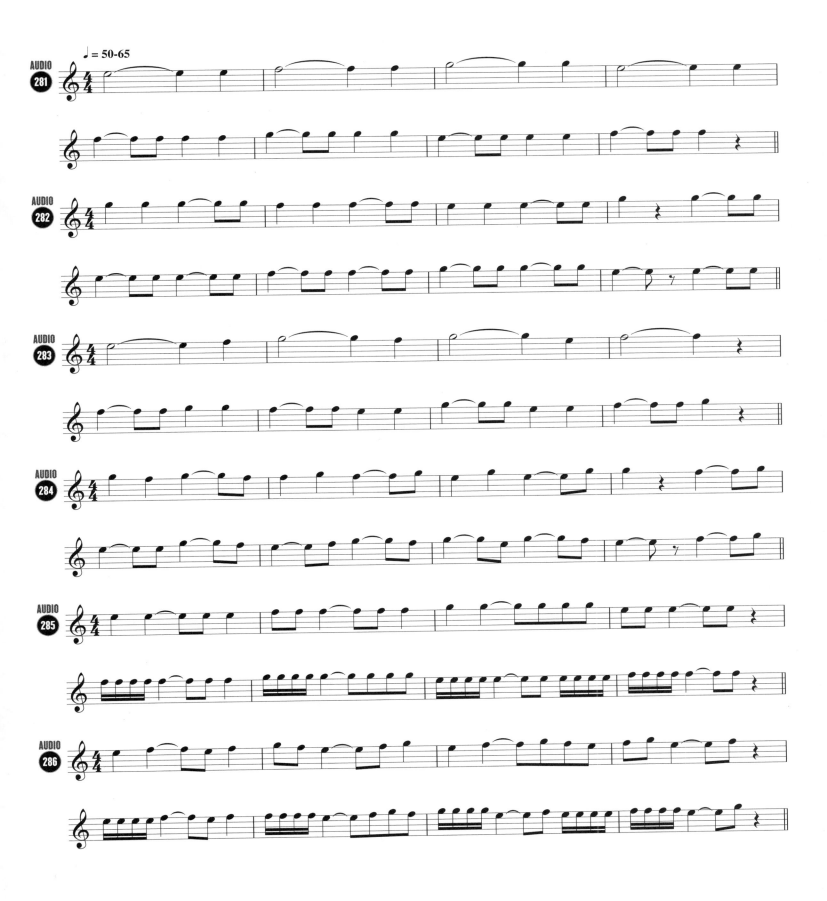

Now here are the same examples (281–296) written in conventional notation.

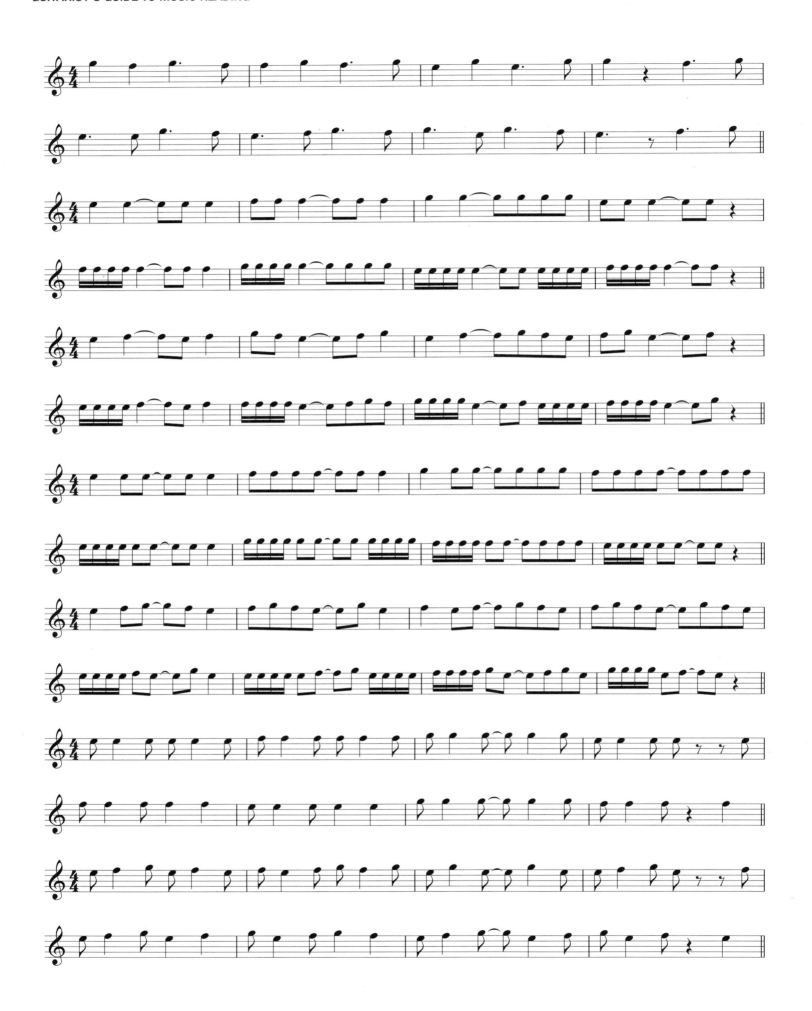

Putting It All Together

Now it's time to take all that you've been working on in this chapter and put it into practice. Throughout the following set of passages you'll encounter shortened note durations by way of staccato markings and extended durations via dots and ties. These should be read in 4th and 5th positions, where Note Groups 1, 2, and 5 are combined, like so:

NOTE GROUPS 1, 2, and 5 in POSITION IV/V

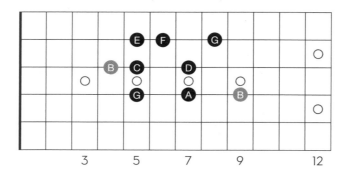

The challenge here is twofold: This is the first time you have multiple duration-altering notation components coming at you, *and* you have to make the call on where to play B. Both challenges demand a single imperative: You *must* read ahead. When it comes to making the call over which B to play, there are no right or wrong answers, but being able to see what's coming will help you in making your decision. If you find the reading is a bit of a "train wreck" (common moniker given to a failed attempt at reading down a chart), then by way of unison position shifting descend down the neck to the open position and play this coalition of Note Groups 1, 2, and 5 there.

NOTE GROUPS 1, 2, and 5 in OPEN POSITION

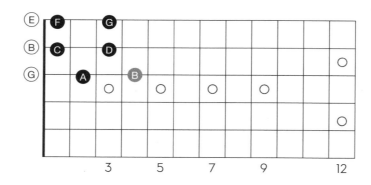

Set your metronome on the low side of 50–65 bpm (even lower if necessary) the first time you read the following passages and try your best not to stop. Play as much as you can in each bar and then break off so you can look ahead to the first beat of the following bar. That will help you keep your place while still working your looking-ahead skills. The two biggest nightmares any reader faces are 1) having to stop, and 2) consequently getting lost while playing with a group. But, that's not going to happen here, because if you've made it to this point you should possess some serious recognition and reaction skills and everything that goes with them!

With all the rhythmic enhancements this chapter introduces, it's important to get as much reading in as you can. Composing your own passages to give yourself more fresh material to read takes on an even greater role, given the frequency with which you'll encounter the essential notation components introduced here and in the next chapter.

CHAPTER 8

Essential Notation Components, Part 2

Continuing your quest to master the skill of music reading, this chapter introduces a new note group containing notes that fall *beneath* the staff, further essential notation components in the form of *accidentals*, and the use of *key signatures*. Let's do it!

Note Group 6: D–E–F

Back in Chapter 4, Note Groups 2 and 3 introduced notes that occupy the spaces and ledger lines *above* the staff.

Now it's time to explore the space *beneath* the staff. Note Group 6 contains the notes D–E–F, with the D note occupying the "borderline" space immediately below the bottom line.

Note D with Tab   **Note E with Tab**   **Note F with Tab**

And here they are in linear fashion, with accompanying tablature, to show you how to play these pitches in the open position on the fourth string.

As you did with other Note Groups, note the stepwise pattern from D to F (and vice versa), which is space–line–space.

Working in open position and using all downstrokes, play the following passages with your metronome set in the range of 50–65 bpm. As you work through these passages, try to read by relationship and not just notes. See the patterned flow of steps while trying to read ahead—preferably in multi-note chunks.

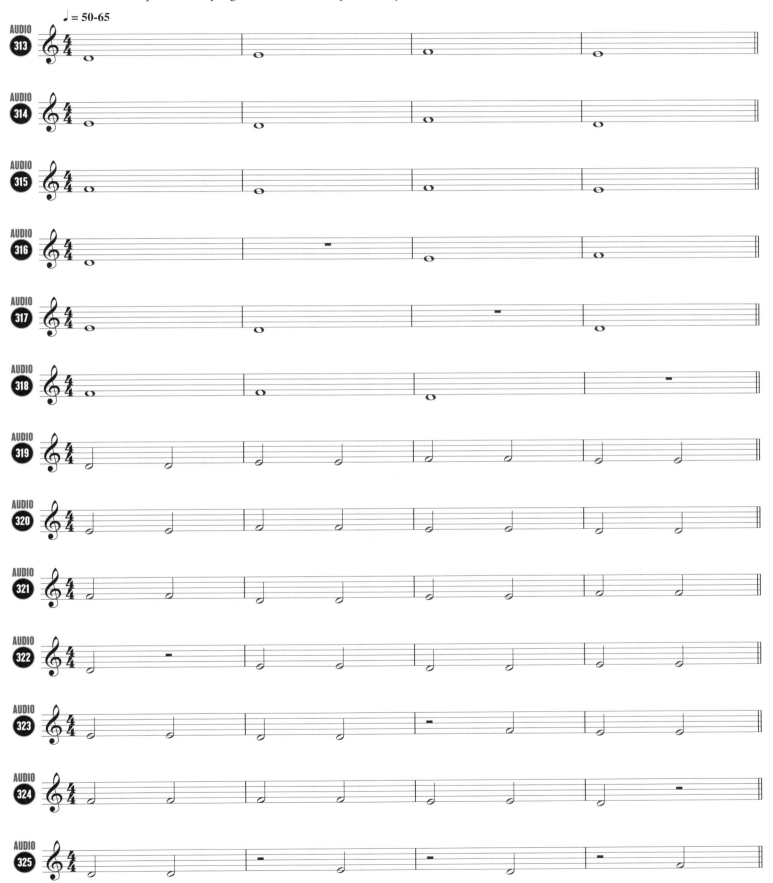

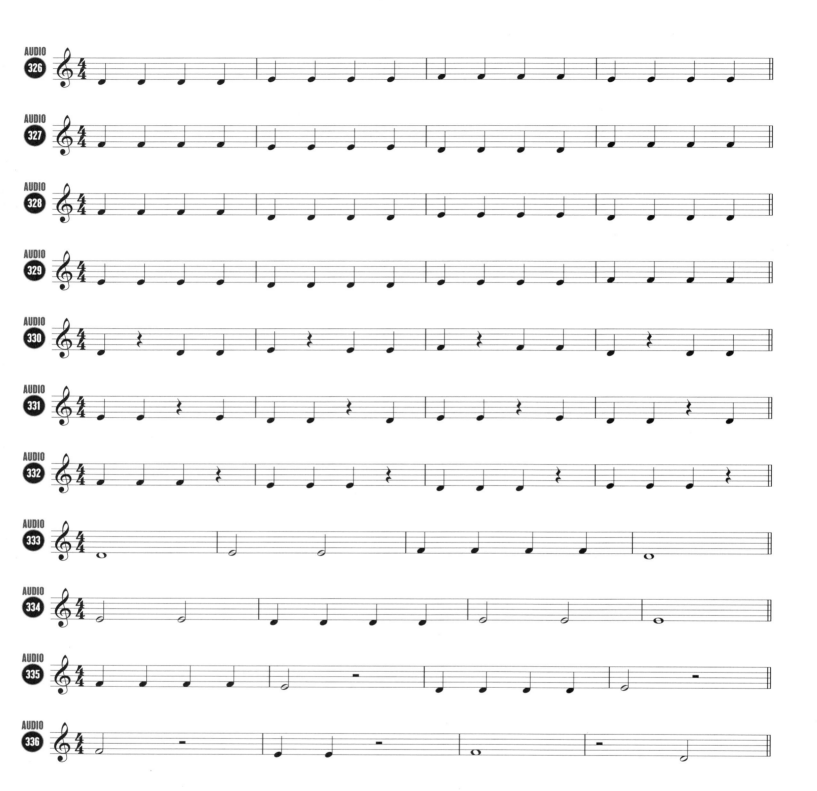

DID YOU KNOW?

This intervallic structure (1–2–♭3) of Note Group 6 is the beginning of several minor scales, including Aeolian (or natural minor), Dorian, harmonic minor, and melodic minor!

When you've made your rounds recycling these passages (which should include unison position shifts powered by diagonal movements), it will be time to throw some new essential notation components in the mix. This time they're all about pitch.

Accidentals

Until now you've been reading unaltered notes, but it's time to change that. *Accidentals* are essential notation components, or symbols, used to raise or lower a note by a half step. There are three types of accidentals: sharp, flat, and natural. When an accidental is used to alter a given note, it will appear immediately to the left of the notehead, like this:

Their functions are simple: a sharp symbol (♯) *raises* the pitch a half step, a flat symbol (♭) *lowers* the pitch by a half step, and a natural symbol (♮) *cancels* a previously placed sharp or flat.

Here are some must-know reading rules for accidentals:

- Accidentals only apply to the octave in which they were written.

- Accidentals remain in effect only in the measure in which they appear.

- A different accidental used on an already altered pitch within the same bar supersedes the previous one.

- Accidentals applied to notes that are tied across bar lines remain in effect until the combined note duration is complete.

In the example above, you might wonder if the second A note in bar two should be played as A♯, because of the tied note at the beginning of the bar, or A natural, as per the second rule of accidentals listed above. Same for the second G in bar 3—is it played G♯ because of the G♯ accidental on beat 2, or is it G natural, because of rule 1 above regarding octaves?

To help you make those calls, you will more often than not see *courtesy accidentals* used in these situations. The courtesy accidental, which may or may not appear in parentheses (as shown below), help remind you of things like an accidental's octave range and bar line limitations.

Now, before you begin reading passages with accidentals, we're going to introduce a variation on Note Group 6—one that includes a sharp note, to help facilitate reading practice with accidentals.

Note Group 6a: D–E–F♯

The next three Note Groups comprise variations on Note Group 6, with accidentals inserted—including natural signs that negate whatever sharp or flat sign you come across *within the same measure*. Remember, once the measure is over, so is the effect of the accidental.

The first variation is seen here in Note Group 6a, in which the third note, F, is raised a half step to F♯.

Whereas the D–E–F sequence you learned earlier marked the first three notes of a D minor scale, raising the 3rd to F♯ makes this trio the start of a D *major* scale. Here's D, E, and F♯ in a linear view, shown horizontally on the staff with accompanying tablature so you can see the slight fingering adjustment in context.

Staying on the D string in the open position, play the following passages with your metronome set between 50–65 bpm. Watch for the insertion of natural sign accidentals and remember the aforementioned measure line rule. At the same time, be mindful that the rhythmic and melodic patterns that initial Note Group passages have followed up until this point will change and remain in effect for the rest of the chapter. Yes, it's time to shake things up a bit!

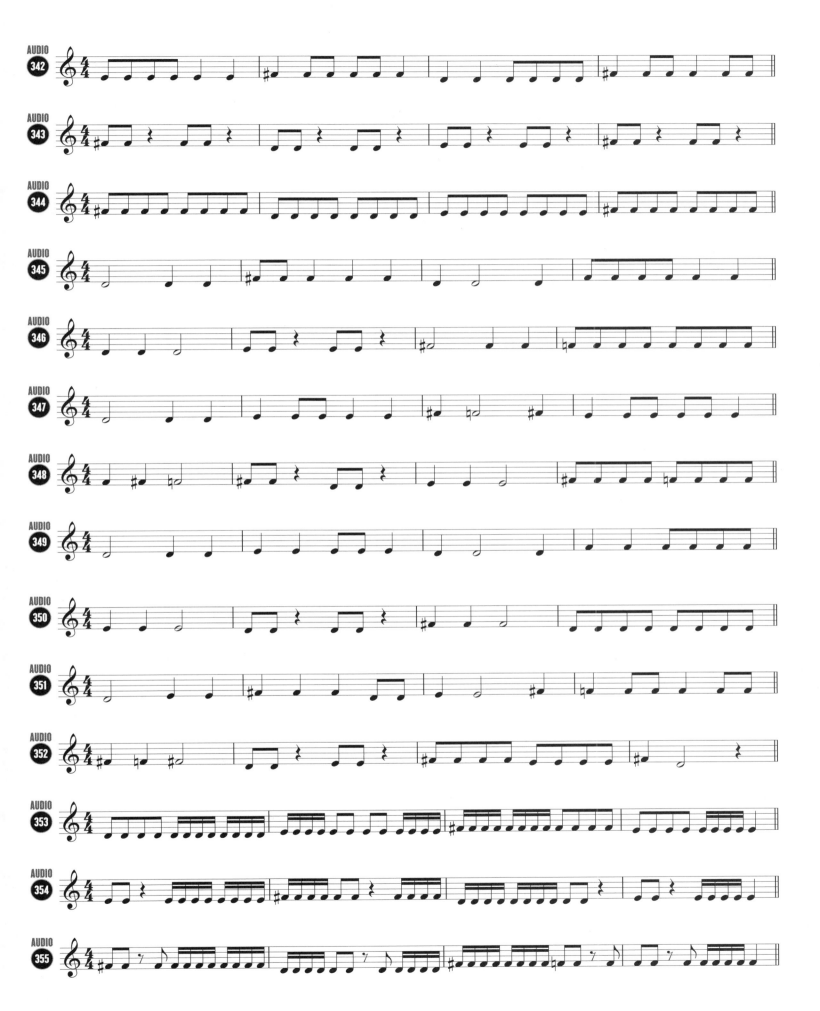

Note Group 6b: D♭–E♭–F

The next variation on Note Group 6 contains a pair of flatted notes, D♭ and E♭, and takes the F back to its "natural" pitch.

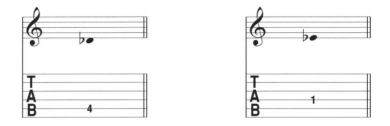

Like the previous variation, this group takes on a major feel, as D♭–E♭–F are the first three notes, or *degrees*, of the D♭ major scale. Here they are together on the staff with accompanying tablature.

Because the D♭ must be played on the 5th string, Note Group 6b is read in 1st position. These are adjustments you'll need to be prepared to make when reading accidentals. As you can see, open position sometimes is the most treacherous when it comes to flatted notes since you can't just lower it a half step. That being said, any natural D note you come upon in the passages ahead should be played on the open D string. It's these sorts of adjustments that will make you appreciate the importance of reading ahead, even if it's just a note or two. You'll want to recognize these variables as early as possible to perform the musical passage without a hitch.

Play the following passages with your metronome set between 50–65 bpm.

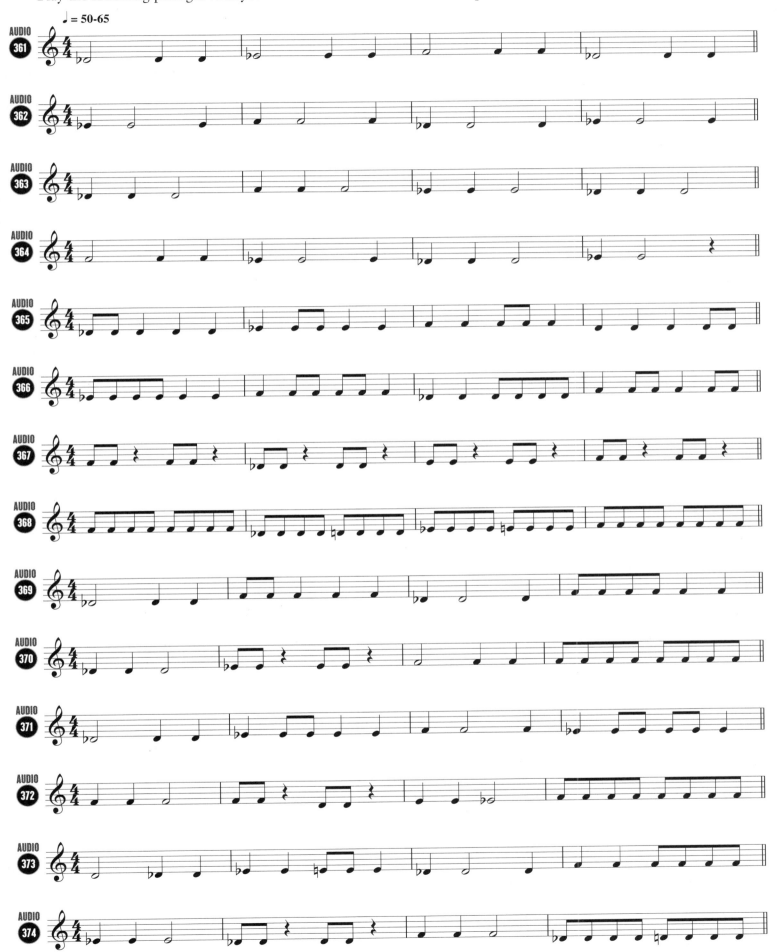

Note Group 6c: D–E♭–F♯

The next variation, Note Group 6c, throws both a sharp and a flat into the mix: D–E♭–F♯. Those of you with a solid grasp of music theory and scales may recognize this intervallic structure as the first three notes of the D Phrygian Dominant scale—the fifth mode of harmonic minor. Here are those notes accompanied by their tab locations.

With the open D now back in the mix along with the 1-1/2 steps between the E♭ and F♯ notes, the following passages are sort of a hybrid of open and 1st position. Use your first and fourth fingers on the E♭ and F♯ notes, respectively, to comfortably make the stretch. Of course, you can always diagonally shift the Note Group to 5th position on the 5th string or even 10th position with the D on the 6th string.

Keeping that metronome set at 50–65 bpm, read these passages down like a pro. Don't forget to watch for natural signs as well as the sharps and flats.

Just like the essential rhythmic components presented in the previous chapter, accidentals require plenty of time and attention at first. Dedicate some of that time to composing your own passages so you can have all the material your head and hands need to learn how to read accidentals with ease. When you're ready to move on, we'll check out how key signatures affect the rules of reading with accidentals.

Key Signatures

When you look at a piece of sheet music, you'll typically see a batch of accidentals placed between the treble clef and time signature; this is called a *key signature*. In short, the key signature tells you which notes should be played sharp, flat, or natural throughout the entire piece. As such, when you're reading "in key," the previously stated list of must-know notational rules change a bit.

- The notes that are sharped or flatted in the key signature are to be played accordingly *every time* you come upon them, regardless of the octave or measure lines.

- Natural signs used to reverse a key signature accidental, or otherwise, still only effect the note within the octave range it was applied and remains in effect only within the measure it was written.

- Accidentals that alter notes outside the key signature follow the previously stated rules.

Now let's see this in action. Taking off from the final passage in Chapter 6, here's an eight-bar exercise that makes use of all the notes in a one-octave cell.

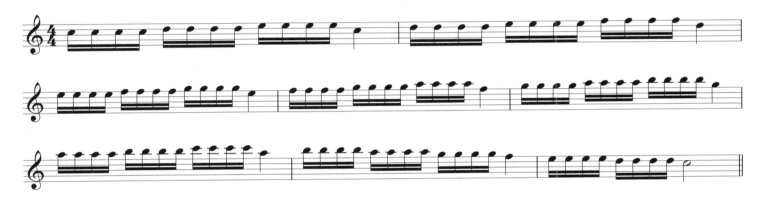

The following 14 eight-bar passages will take the above example in C and *transpose*, or change, it to all the other keys. Remember, any sharp or flat symbol that appears in the key signature indicates that note should be played sharp or flat for the entire duration of the piece. For example, in the first one (the key of G), the top line (F note) has a sharp symbol on it, meaning that every time you see an F note, you should play it as F♯, regardless of which octave it appears in. Likewise, in the key of D that follows, every F and C note is played as F♯ and C♯, respectively.

Sharp Keys

Key of G

Key of D

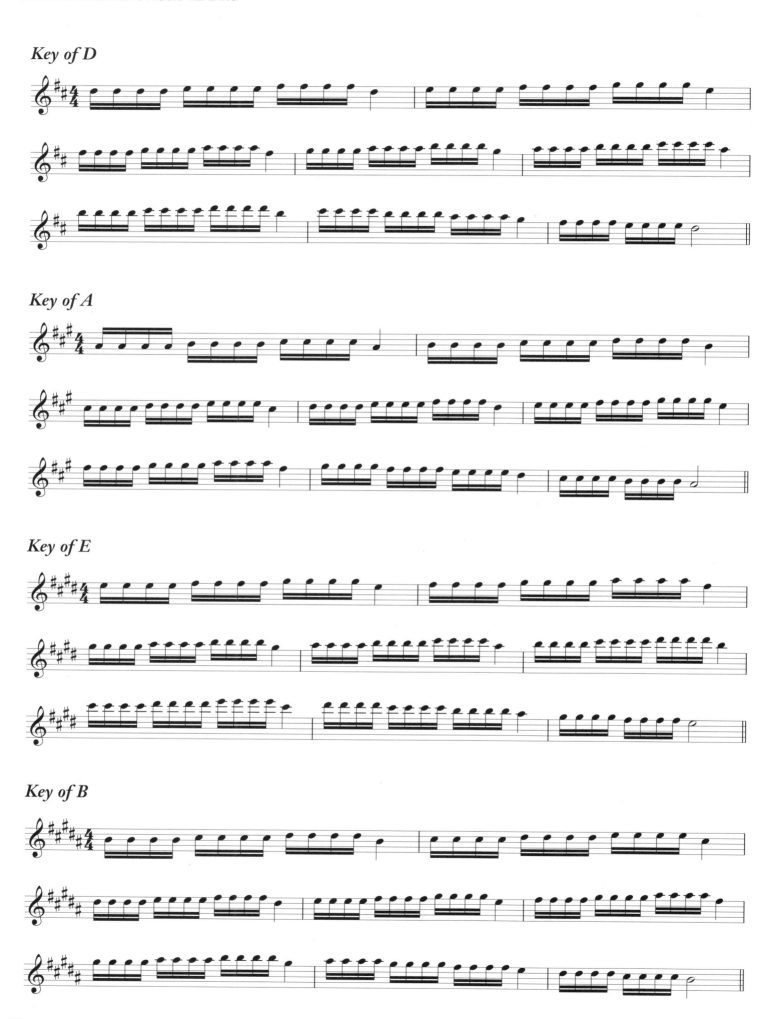

Key of A

Key of E

Key of B

Key of F#

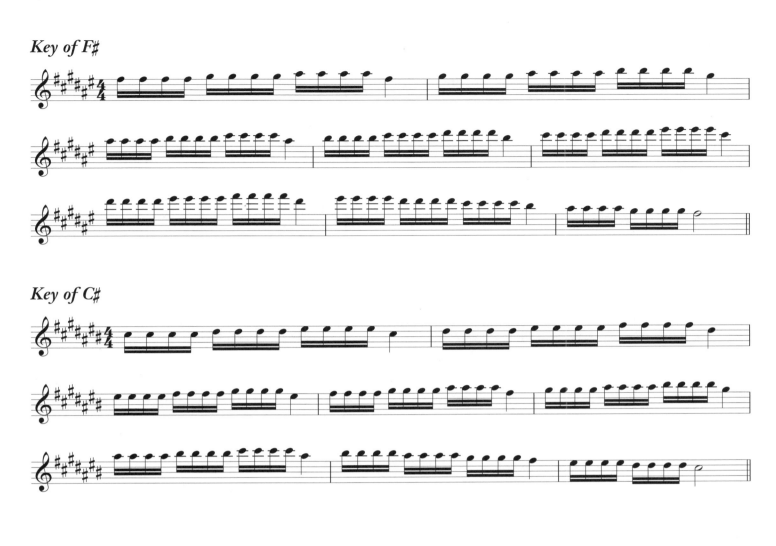

Key of C#

Flat Keys

Key of F

Key of B♭

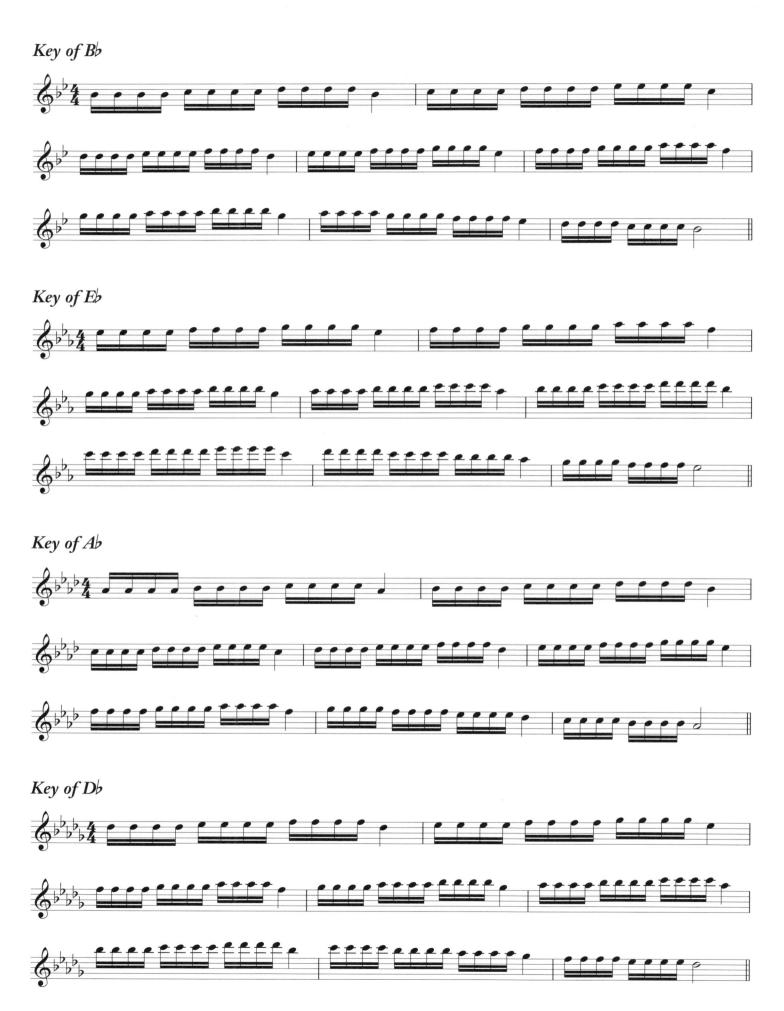

Key of E♭

Key of A♭

Key of D♭

Key of G♭

Key of C♭

So, are you ready to play these? What? Think you can't do it? Read the next chapter, then come back to these passages, and you'll read them with ease—trust me.

CHAPTER 9

Reading by Degree

For the entirety of the book so far, you've been working on developing recognition and reaction skills pertaining to what's literally on the paper. Whether notes, rhythms, or motives made up of one or both elements, the goal has been to develop approaches that allow you to read on guitar as best you can.

This chapter, however, introduces a concept where you'll read what's on the paper—but as something all together different that allows you to read what's actually *not* there at all! How? Reading by degree, that's how.

Scale Degrees vs. Intervals

When I say "reading by degree," I mean reading by *scale degree*. What I'm about to hip you to is reading notes *not* as notes, but as *numbers*. To fully understand this concept, we first need to address the confusion between *scale degrees* and *intervals*. Although they can be interpreted as the same thing—and sometimes that's correct—they are in fact different. Let's see how by starting with two simple definitions:

- *Scale degrees* are the numerical placement of the note in a scale.

- An *interval* is the distance between two notes.

Looking at the figure below we see two notes—G and B—in the key of G major:

The distance between these two notes, or the *interval*, is a 3rd, or to be more exact, a major 3rd. In terms of scale degrees, B is the 3rd note of the scale or simply "3." Right now the interval and the scale degree designation is the same. Now take B and raise it an octave:

The interval between G and this B is a 10th, but the scale degree designation does not change; B is still a 3. Here's one more: Take that B and lower it two octaves so its pitch range is actually below G:

In order to formulate the interval, you now have to consider B as the root key, which makes this pair a minor 6th. But, check it out: This figure is still in G and that B is *still* a 3 in terms of scale degrees! This makes the scale degree a movable entity, whereas the interval is a stationary one. As a result, scale degrees are much more flexible.

Since scale degrees have fixed numerical assignments, the system never changes *and* it allows you to look at every scale with *one set of numbers*. For example, whether you're in major, minor, or somewhere in between, the root will *always* be the first degree or "1." This is how scale degrees allow you not only to read notes as numbers—making melodic motives that much easier to detect, regardless of the key—but also serve as a very effective method for transposing what's on the paper, thus playing notes that are *not even there*.

Reciting and Reading Scale Degree Designations

A great way to get the concept of reading by degree off and running is to recite the scale degree designations before you read a note, not unlike the tapping exercises you did when learning to read rhythms. For example, let's revisit the one-octave cell passage in C from the end of the previous chapter, only this time I've added the scale degree designations below the staff.

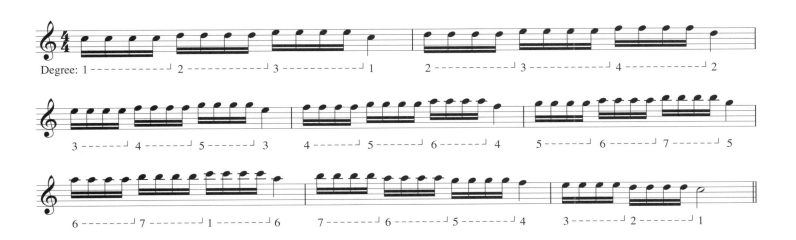

Now it's your turn. The following passages all stay within that one-octave cell range. First read them by degree (don't actually play), reciting each scale step as you go. Then play them with scale degree designations as your focus. You may want to take some time to associate all this degree numerology with your budding neck vision skills, keeping these tips in mind.

- Say the degrees as you play the cell.

- Break up the scale cell as you continue, to associate the degrees with what you're playing.

- As you get more comfortable, take your eyes off the neck to help learn the feel of where the degrees are.

Ready? Set your metronome between 50–65 bpm and be sure to read ahead, look for motives, and don't stop.

Be sure to follow that up with some recycling methods such as reading backwards, turning the book over, and reading down the page instead of across it.

Now it's time to really put this concept to the test. The next set of passages are the same ones you just recited and read, but in different keys and reordered. Do the same here: Recite the scale degree designations and then read them down. To move the cell, all you have to do is move it up or down the neck so that the root note on the G string matches up with the key that the passage is in, and you're good to go.

Key of G

Key of D

Key of A

Key of E

Key of B

Key of F♯

Key of C♯

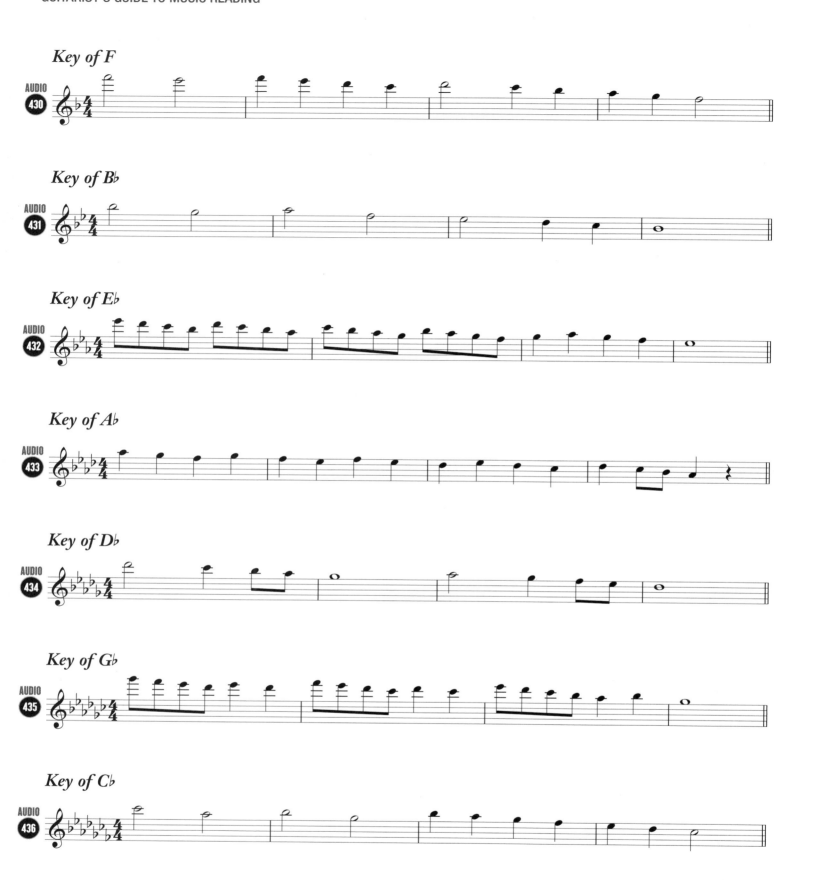

Now that you've finished here, go back and read down those passages at the end Chapter 8—the ones I said would later be done with ease. It will, just wait and see!

Transposing

One of the most revered reading techniques is transposing on sight, where the reader plays what's on the paper but in a different key, on the spot. Although that may sound beyond your skills at this point, with a solid foundation in reading by degree and starting out slow and simple, you can do it.

You can give transposing a go by going back and reading down all the passages composed using Note Groups 1–6. Simply assign the lowest note as "1" and the next two as "2" and "3," respectively. Keep the whole/half step structure of the groups intact and don't concern yourself with degree designation in regards to any stated diatonic. Aside from Note Groups 1 and 2, all the step sequences are unique. When you start to recite the scale degree designations you'll discover the purposeful intent that I was prepping you for all along with regard to scale degree progression—they're all the same!

Be patient and give this time to set in. When it does, it's extremely empowering.

CHAPTER 10

Essential Notation Components, Part 3

Looking once more at a set of notational components essential to effectively reading music, this chapter gets into pickup notes, repeat signs, and properly reading in different octave ranges while revisiting ledger lines—this time going down below the staff. You'll explore these components through three new Note Groups, two of which will be introduced in a descending order.

Note Group 7: Lower Ledger Lines: C–B–A

Note Group 7 takes you on your first journey to ledger lines that fall below the staff, beginning right under the D on the lower "borderline" space. To give you a mental advantage, this Note Group is presented in descending order, starting with C on the first ledger line below the staff.

Note C with Tab   **Note B with Tab**   **Note A with Tab**

Here they are in a single musical system, so you can see the descending ledger line-space-line pattern more easily.

In open position with a suggested approach of all downstrokes, play the following passages with your metronome set to 50–65 bpm. Note that starting on C, on the first ledger line below the staff, is the mirror image of Chapter 4's Note Group 3 that started on A on the first ledger line *above* the staff. The purpose is to make use of the same logic, where you gradually progressed in ledger line count as you learned them.

As you go back and recycle the previous passages, be sure to add a pass of reading by degree. But when you do, consider this: There are two ways to interpret them.

> A = 1 (tonic)
>
> B = 2nd
>
> C = 3rd

Or:

> C = 1 (tonic)
>
> B = 7th
>
> A = 6th

My suggestion? Try them both! Besides helping you decide on an approach when faced with this scenario on a real gig, it gives you the opportunity to recycle the same material in yet another way, giving you even more reading practice.

Pickup Notes

Oftentimes when reading a new piece of music, you'll find that it starts with what seems like an incomplete measure. It's not a mistake; rather, it's a *pickup measure*, or more formerly, an *anacrusis*. Pickups are a sequence of notes that precede the first downbeat of the first complete bar of music, as seen in this example.

WHAT'S WITH THE "BIRD'S EYE?"

Right above the second quarter note in the sixth bar you'll see a notational symbol that looks sort of like a bird's eye (𝄐). This is called a *fermata*. It signals the reader to hold the note for a longer duration than its actual note value. That duration is left up to the player or person leading the band or ensemble. You *might* see a fermata above a rest or bar line, indicating an indefinite pause, but mostly you will see them above notes as you further your reading.

The next set of passages will continue to make use of Note Group 7, since beginning readers are famously weak with ledger lines. That's also why there were some extra passages when this group was first introduced. You'll find a pickup at the onset of every one. To determine when to start playing the pickup note(s), simply look at the combined values of the pickup and count backwards—where you stop is where you'll start playing when you count yourself in. Be mindful that sometimes you'll need to come in on an upbeat.

Let's do that again, only this time we'll mix in some accidentals.

Take this idea of transforming passages and run with it when composing your own reading material to recycle.

Note Group 8: Lower Ledger Lines G–F–E

Note Group 8 presents a unique reading environment; that is, there's only one location on the neck to read this range of notes E, F, and G!

Note G with Tab   Note F with Tab   Note E with Tab

Following the same descending order as Note Group 7, let's look at G, F, and E in a linear view on the staff and set in the open position, as seen in the tablature.

The staff pattern flow here is ledger space–ledger line–ledger space, with the low E representing the bottom of the guitar's range in standard tuning. Since beginning readers typically experience some trouble with ledger lines, and you don't have the opportunity to make use of diagonal movements and unison position shifts, I've provided plenty of opportunity to read down passages with Note Group 8. But first, we're going to explore reading with repeat signs.

Repeat Signs

Repeat signs do just what the phrase implies—they instruct the reader to play something at least one more time, if not more. Repeat signs, or brackets, are shown as a terminal double bar line, with two dots (like a colon) on the "note side." Any music within those borders—be it a single measure or an entire section—should be immediately repeated one time.

When the selected passage is to be repeated more than once, the number of repeats will be indicated above the final bar.

Now, let's get to the Note Group 8 passages. Playing on the low E string in the open position with a suggested approach of all downstrokes, play the following passages with your metronome set at 50–65 bpm. You'll start out reading G on the second ledger space below the staff and gradually increase the ledger line count as you progress. Be sure to watch for repeat signs as well as instructions to repeat more than once!

REPEAT BRACKET SHORTHAND

Occasionally you may see just one repeat bracket (an ending one) somewhere after the start of the music. This means you are to repeat everything from the beginning of the piece up until that bracket. If the bracket is at the very end, then you're to play the entire piece again.

Also when you're directed to repeat more than once, you may see the signification shortened to simply *4x* as opposed to *Play 4 times*.

Repeat Endings

Repeat endings are used when the repeated sections have two or more different endings. In the example here, you would play the first four bars (the music between the repeat signs) once, then repeat just the first three measures and skip to the second ending.

Playing again on the low E string in the open position and sticking with all the guidelines outlined thus far, play the following passages and keep an eye out for repeat endings.

Single and Double Measure Repeats

There are other more informal repeat signs you should be familiar with. A *single measure repeat* instructs you to repeat the measure immediately preceding it, in its entirety.

Double measure repeats tell us to play the two previous measures in their entirety. With double measure repeats, a numeral "2" may or may not appear above the staff.

This is more of a shorthand notation method that you're more likely to see on handwritten charts from a bandleader than you will on published sheet music. Regardless, it's a must-know notation tool. Following are some more passages using Note Group 8, with single and double repeats added.

Repeat Sign Terms to Know

Before we close this section on repeat signs, there's some more terminology and symbols you need to know regarding repeats. These are used to direct you back to specific points in the music or to jump ahead to a particular measure that would be otherwise impossible to convey using repeat brackets or endings.

Da Capo

Abbreviated *D.C.*, this means in Italian to play "from the beginning." It's basically the same as a single repeat bracket found at the end of piece.

Dal Segno

Abbreviated *D.S.*, this means in Italian to play "from the sign," which means to go back to the sign 𝄋. So in the passage below, you would play the first six bars, then return to bar 3 and play through to the end.

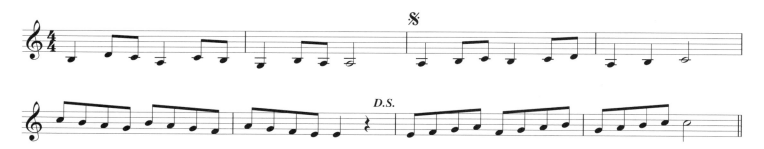

al fine

Both D.C. and D.S. are often accompanied by modifying instructions, one of which is *al fine*, which means in Italian, "to the end." So in the following passage, you would play the first six bars, return to the beginning of the piece, and then play through to the end. Sometimes, though, the end is *not* the end. In this case, you will see the word *Fine* above the staff, and you would end the piece at that point.

al Coda

D.C. and D.S. can also be modified with *al Coda*. A Coda is a section of music that's regarded as a "tail" to the main body. It's represented by this symbol ⊕, which resembles a cross hair within a capital letter "O." The *al Coda* instruction means that after going back to either the beginning (D.C.) or the sign (D.S.), you continue to the Coda sign, at which point you jump ahead to the Coda section.

Following are some longer passages that utilize all of the repeat terminology just introduced. You'll be reading from Note Groups 7 and 8 in the open position, between 50–65 bpm. There will also be some light syncopation as well as essential rhythmic components from Chapter 7. Stay sharp and read ahead!

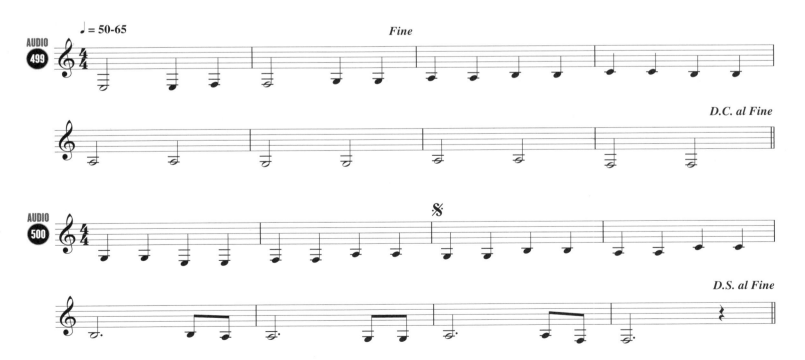

Note Group 9: 12th Position E–F–G

Switching gears, Note Group 9 contains the same notes as Note Group 8, only the pitch range is three octaves higher, placing Note Group 9 on ledger lines *above* the staff, higher than you've read thus far!

Note E with Tab   Note F with Tab   Note G with Tab

Beginning on the third ledger line above the staff, Note Group 9 follows a ledger line–ledger space–ledger line pattern, as seen below in linear fashion, in 12th position.

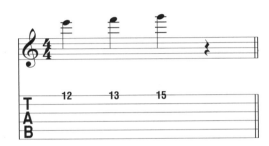

This Note Group can be moved, using unison position shifts, up to 17th position on the B string on standard 21- or 22-fret necks, and for those who have a 24-fret neck, it can go all the way up to 21st position on the G string.

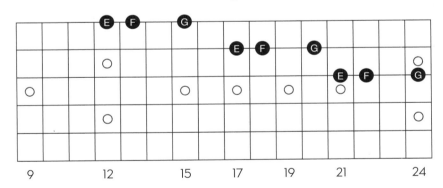

Play the following passages in 12th position on the high E string with your metronome set between 50–65 bpm (I suggest the lower tempo range, both to have the best opportunity to read ahead and to help get familiar with the higher ledger line count). From there, make the shifts to the other positions, but not before exercising the various recycling methods in this position.

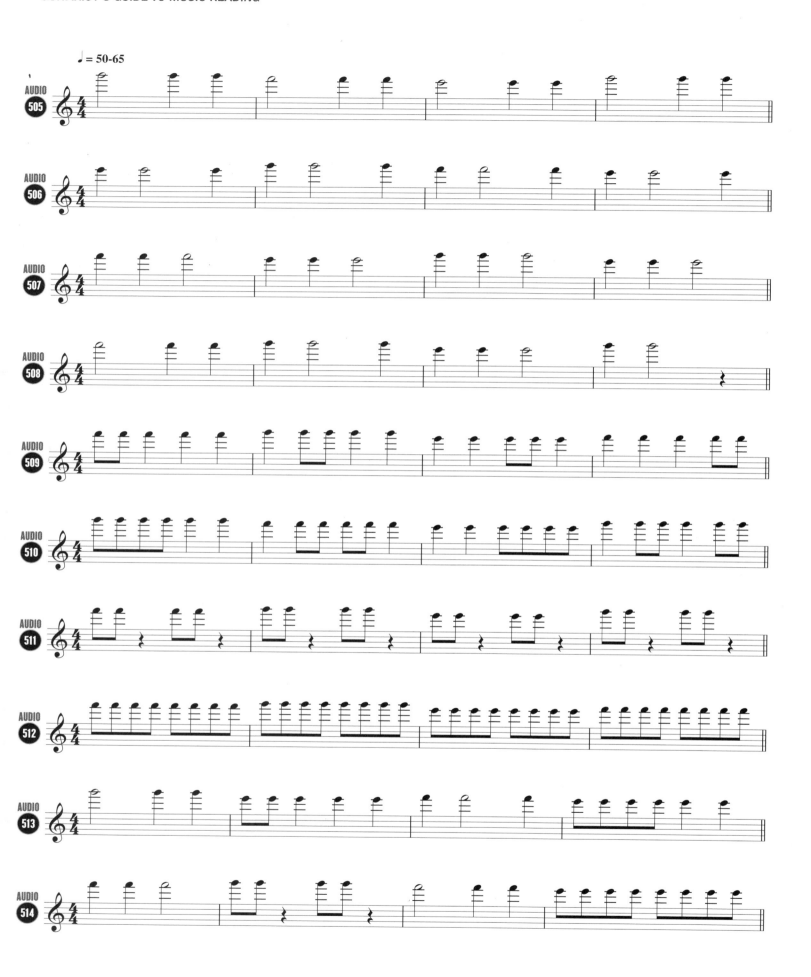

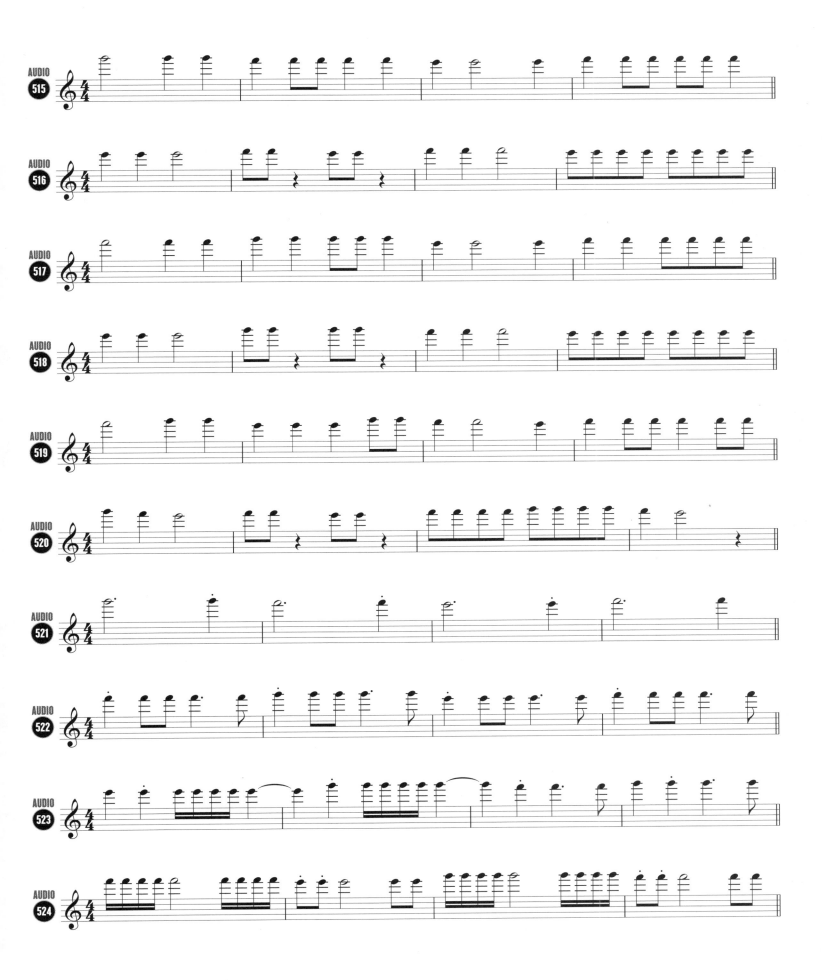

THE FORGOTTEN "D"

Somewhere within the nine Note Groups that have been studied, this range of D has escaped us:

While the preceding passages made use of Note Group 9 exclusively, you'll read this range of D later in the final two chapters.

The Octava

As you just experienced, reading notes on high ledger lines can be a bit difficult. So to make reading pitch in the higher ranges more manageable, you'll sometimes see an *octava* symbol (*8va*), which is an essential notation component that instructs the reader to play an octave above the written pitch. For example, with an *8va* present, you might be reading in Note Group 2's range, but actually playing in Note Group 9's range.

The next set of passages will dive right in and have you raising Note Groups 1–8 up an octave. To begin, simply raise them up to 12th position. Stay sharp, though, as all the essential notation components explored in these last few chapters will come at you. As usual, set your metronome at a comfortable tempo between 50–65 bpm, making sure you can read ahead. And remember: don't stop! Recycle at will.

8vb

Just as the *8va* symbol instructs you to play an octave above the written pitch, the *8vb* symbol directs you to play an octave below the written notation.

CHAPTER 11

Establishing Rhythm Recognition Skills | The Power of the Triplet

Up until this point, you've been reading within even numbers with regard to rhythm. From meters to subdivisions, it's all been divisible by two and usually in sets of four. This chapter takes you to another common rhythmic environment wherein the elements are divisible by three. We'll first explore various time signatures in compound meters to help you establish a firm rhythmic foundation in the "three feel." Then we'll explore *borrowed metric groupings* and learn about *numbered brackets*. As always, you'll start to develop your rhythm recognition skills for these new rhythmic devices by once again tapping out passages, this time with a "three feel," within the three common *triplet-based groupings*.

Compound Meters

Back in Chapter 1, we established a fundamental understanding of rhythm. You learned that as music moves through time, consistent *pulsations* occur, which in music are called *beats*. You also learned that when beats are organized into a pattern, they're defined by the first beat of the group, which is *stressed*. Those patterns led by the stressed beats are what we now know as *meter*.

And until now, you've been working in the *simple meter*—i.e., a meter that divides evenly by two—of "4," which contains one stressed, or strong, beat followed by three weak beats, with the quarter note as the beat unit. While that's the most common meter in contemporary music, it is by no means the only game in town. So now it's time to examine *compound* or *triple meters*, which divide evenly by *three* and also further divide the pulse into three beats.

Besides the obvious change—odd vs. even numbers—the key point here is that the pulses that make up the meter can, and usually are, further *divided* into sets of three. Take a look at this next passage.

The time signature is 3/4, which indicates a meter of "three" (top number) with a quarter note (bottom number) as the beat unit; in other words, three quarter notes per bar. According to the tempo marking, you're to feel each pulse as a whole at 120 bpm, making this example clearly showcase the first dimension of compound meters, where the beat group organization defined by stress is three (hence the "1-2-3" count underneath the passage).

But what about that second dimension, where the beats themselves are divided into three? That brings us to the idea of...

Dotted Beat Units

Let's look at the same passage, this time with a new beat unit—an eighth note—receiving one beat.

So now we're in 3/8 time, where every *eighth* note receives one beat (as reflected in the tempo marking). But because we changed both the tempo marking and the time signature (and notice the count stays the same as well), in effect, nothing has changed as to how the passage sounds when played.

To enter the second dimension of compound meter, and thus changing the feel, a *dotted beat unit* is required.

Notice the tempo marking now displays a dotted quarter note. Remember, a dot adds half the value of the note to which it's applied. In this case, a quarter note—universally recognized as one beat that equals two eighth notes—is dotted to make it worth *three eighth notes*. There is now an underlying subdivision feel against the 40 bpm pulse that splits it into three equal parts. Whenever the meter is divisible by three (3, 6, 9, 12, etc.) and the bottom number of the time signature is "8," it nearly always means the underlying rhythm is to be felt as three eighth notes, or triplets, per beat.

This will also influence the count as well. While you'll still hear a three count, the "1" will be stressed (notice how the count below the staff above has "1" in bold) while the following "2" and "3" will follow at a normal volume. Against the underlying pulse the count will be felt in an even group of three. If the time signature were 6/8, you would have two sets of three per bar, like this:

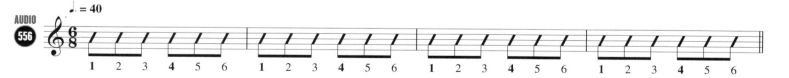

To summarize, you could think of meters divisible by two (and whose pulses are felt as a whole) as one-dimensional, hence the same "simple." In contrast, meters divisible by three, and whose pulses are further divided into groups of three beats, are two-dimensional, thus aptly called "compound." Triple meters whose beat units are not dotted are still felt in three, but it's the compound aspect that really drives the feel home.

Tapping in Groups of Three

In this section you're going to tap out various passages that toggle between simple quadruple (4/4) and simple triple (3/4) meters, and compound triple meters (3/8 and 6/8). Be sure to note the varying tempos from passage to passage. Don't be alarmed by the higher tempos—by now your rhythm recognition and reading-ahead skills can handle these simple, rhythm-only passages at a medium-high tempo range.

Tap out the following four-bar passages while trying to count out the downbeats and the three feel per beat when applicable.

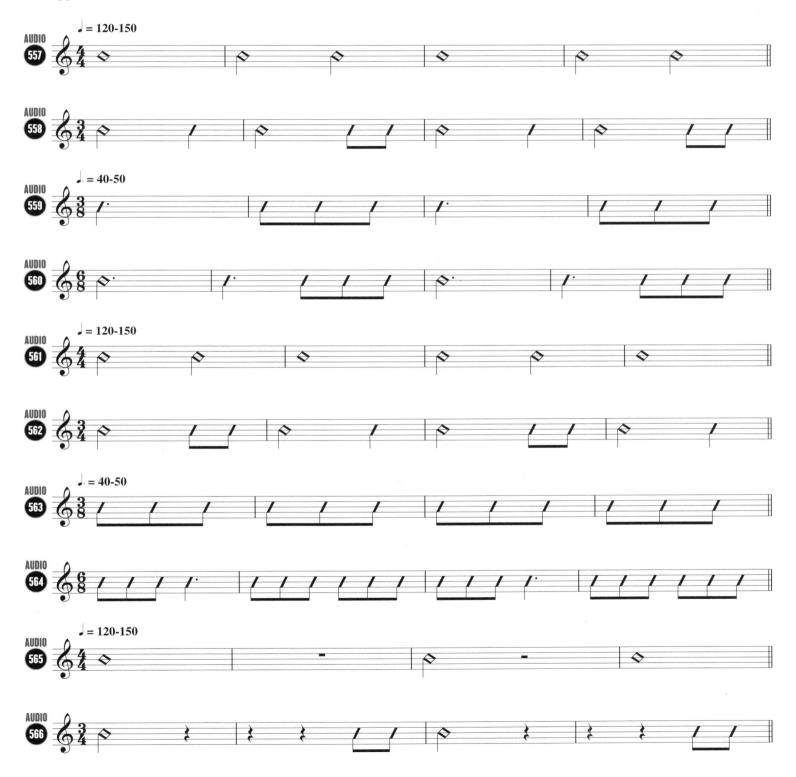

Triplets and Embedded Rests

Back in Chapter 5, we introduced the concept of subdivisions. With a note duration hierarchy that follows "4" as the beat unit, you delved into eighth and sixteenth notes and have since read those rhythms in various syncopations as you've furthered your rhythm and pitch recognition skills. In this chapter, we are returning to subdivisions, only this time using groups of three and compound meters. Enter the *triplet*!

Triplets can and will come up in simple meters. Along with other groupings outside of two (eighth notes) and four (sixteenth notes), these are referred to as *borrowed metric groupings*. Triplets and other borrowed metric groupings are easy to spot as they're always notated with *numbered brackets* (or beams).

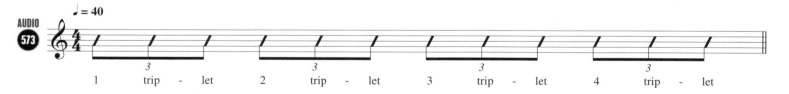

The number "3" immediately below each beam indicates a subdivision of three—in this case, a per-beat division given the quarter note beat unit and the three eighth notes connected by a beam beneath the bracket. In theory, the previous example sounds the same as 12/8 with a dotted quarter note beat unit.

Triplets can comprise more than just eighth notes. The following three sections will explain the ins and outs of recognizing and interpreting each of the three triplet subdivision types and their embedded rests. I call them *embedded* rests, because, as you can see in the next passage, the rests fall under the "umbrella" of the numbered bracket.

For now, the supporting passages will continue to be in 4/4, keeping you in that metric comfort zone, but that will change once the pitch element returns in the next chapter. Be aware of attacks that will *not* be on the downbeat, as this will be needed in order to properly interpret the upbeat swing feel (explained later). Of course, there will be tips on how to count, but the goal is to eventually *feel* the subdivisions while counting the basic pulses within a given meter. Don't forget to recycle and write your own for even more opportunity to read fresh, related material and help you hone these recognition skills!

Eighth-Note Triplets

As stated, a bar of 4/4 with eighth-note triplets feels the same as a bar of 12/8 with a dotted quarter note beat unit. In the following passages, you're going to put that into practice and tap out a plethora of eighth note "trips." It's important that you have a firm grasp on how eighth-note triplets feel, because they serve as the foundation for the next two triplet-based borrowed metric groupings.

Setting your metronome between 50–65 bpm, you can count the triplet instances like so: "**1**-trip-let, **2**-trip-let, etc." Or, you can count them as "trip-a-let" or simply "1-2-3." Keep in mind, though, that the latter approaches may throw you off, as you'll be dropping the metric count. Also, reading ahead becomes even more crucial as you switch between straight eighths and triplets.

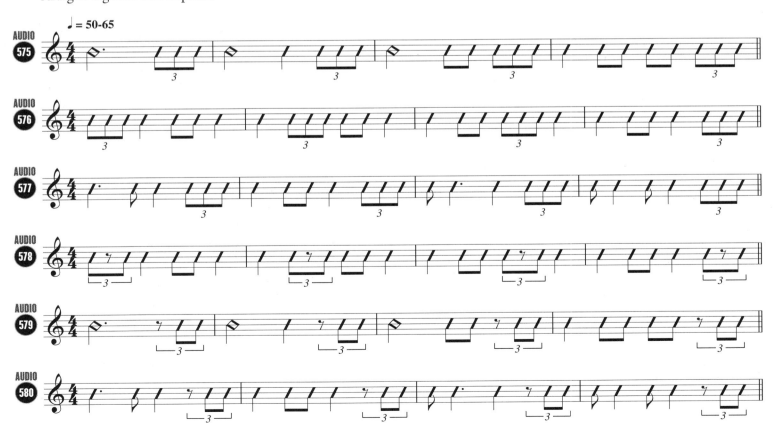

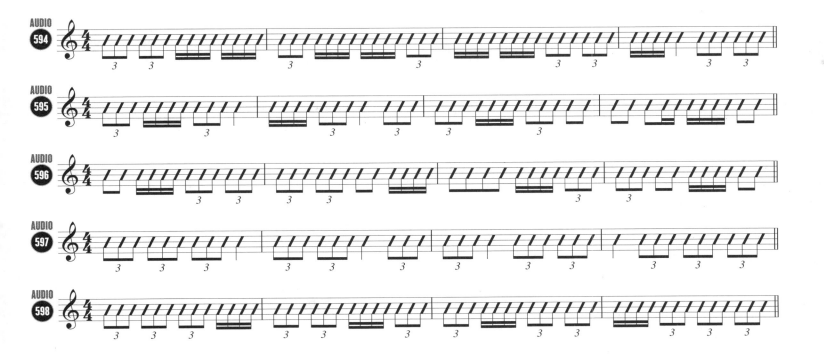

Sixteenth-Note Triplets

Just as straight eighths subdivide into sixteenths, so do eighth-note triplets subdivide into sixteenth-note triplets.

SEXTUPLETS

In the previous example, the notation shows the triplet subdivisions very clearly, using brackets; however, in simple meter like 4/4 time, a single beat containing two sixteenth-note triplets (like beats 1 and 3 above) is almost always written as a *sextuplet*, which indicates six notes in the space of one quarter note beat, as shown here:

When you come across a sextuplet, it's much easier to count it as two sixteenth-note triplets than it is to count to "six." That being said, some educators see a difference, in that a pair of sixteenth-note triplets in the space of one quarter note should contain an accent in the middle (downbeat of the second triplet, or the fourth note of the sextuplet), while the sextuplet should be played straight through with no accent. But for all intents and purposes, you can treat them the same when reading and playing a piece of music.

The easiest way to feel sixteenth note "trips" is to think of them as triplet subdivisions on the downbeat and upbeat. The double beams indicate sixteenth notes, while the numbered brackets remind you they're to be felt as groups of three. That being said, you can apply the same counting approaches discussed in the previous section on both sides of the beat.

Switch your metronome back to the range of 50–65 bpm (you may want to stay on the lower end of the tempo range) and tap the following passages. Note that in passages 606 and 607, you'll see beats containing a sixteenth note followed by two sixteenth rests, another sixteenth note and two more sixteenth rests. Rhythmically, this is identical to a pair of staccato eighth notes, which is how you would see it notated 99.9% of the time. I present it in this format just to help reinforce the triplet subdivisions.

Once again, reading ahead becomes even more crucial, this time so you can see those sixteenth-note triplet instances coming.

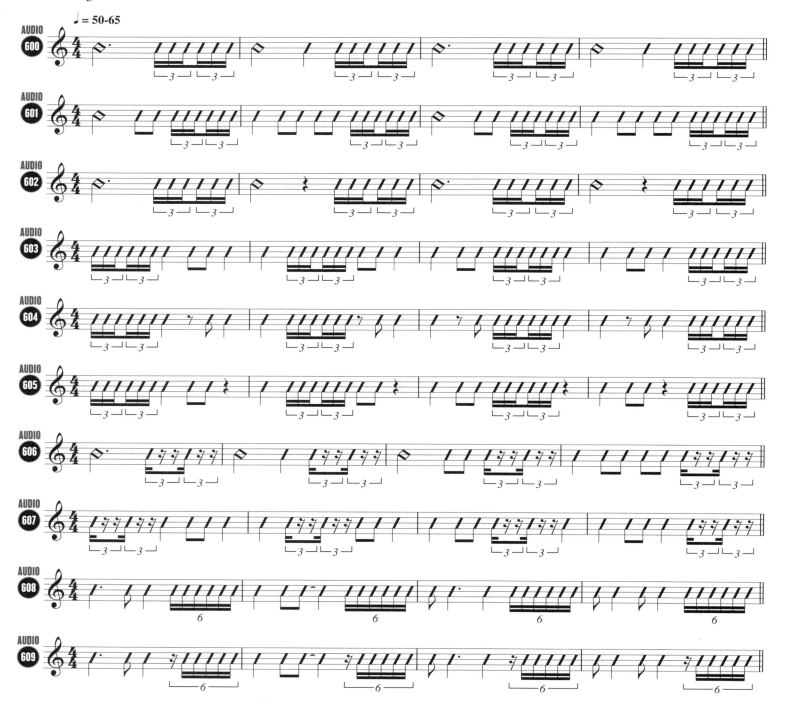

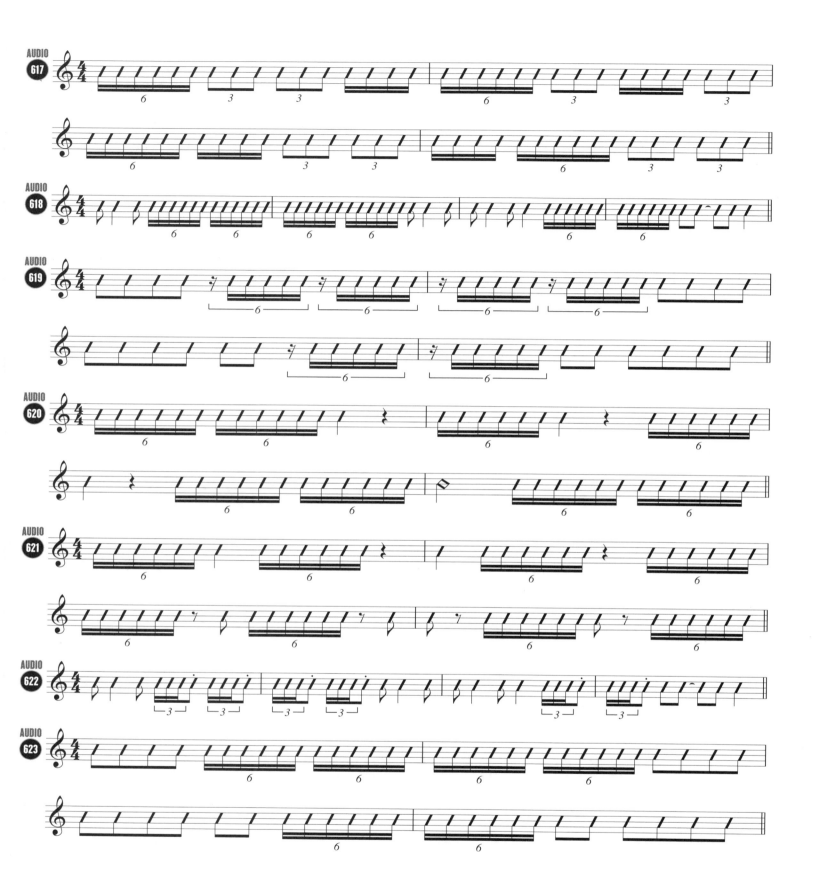

Quarter-Note Triplets

To learn sixteenth-note triplets, we simply doubled up eighth-note triplets. Now, to learn *quarter-note triplets*, we're going to take the opposite route, rhythmically speaking. Whereas the eighth-note triplet splits a single beat into three equal parts, the quarter-note triplet splits *two beats* into three parts. This tends to be a tricky one, but if you use eighth-note triplets as a backdrop, you can rather painlessly learn the feel of quarter-note triplets. Let's take a look at the following passage and examine the count below.

As you can see, the concept of a quarter note is equal to two eighth notes prevails here, just set in a different scenario. When first learning quarter-note triplets, you can use an eighth-note triplet count for two beats playing on the first and third subdivisions of the first eighth-note triplet on beat 1, and on the second subdivision of the eighth-note triplet in beat 2. Put simply, you're attacking a note on every other subdivision of two consecutive eighth-note triplets. It's almost as if you're applying a two-dimensional compound count! If you want to verbally count this out, stress the attacks in the count like this, "**1**-2-**3**, 1-**2**-3" or "**1**-trip-**LET**, 2-**TRIP**-let" or "**TRIP**-a-**LET**, trip-**A**-let."

With a click set to 50–65 bpm (once again you may want to stay on the lower end of the tempo range), tap the following passages while verbalizing the eighth-note triplet count, to help you learn the feel of the quarter-note triplet. Be sure to read ahead so you can adjust your counting accordingly.

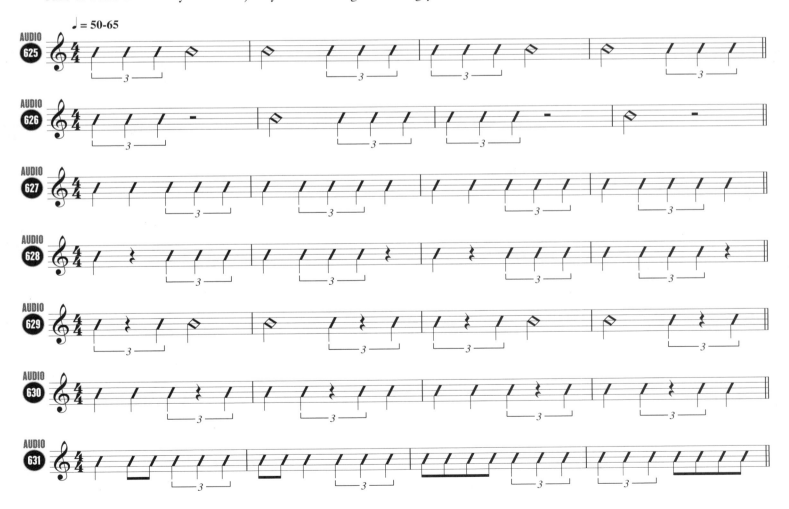

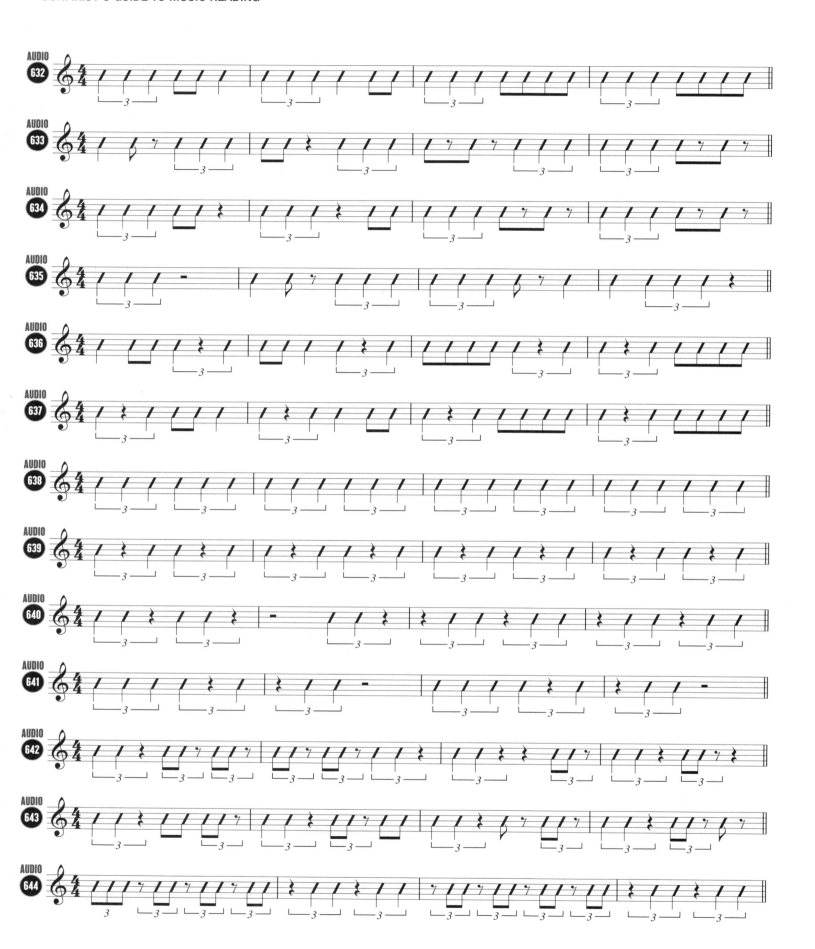

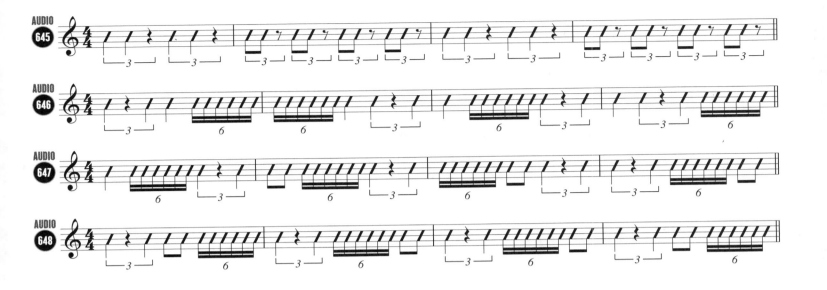

CHAPTER 12

Next Level Time Signatures

Throughout this book, you've learned concepts that help not only to read guitar music but also bridge the gap between neck and notation. You've worked to develop rhythm- and pitch-recognition skills as well as neck vision skills through diagonal movements, unison position shifts, and other vision-based concepts, and even discovered ways to recycle written music so you can constantly read the ever-important fresh material. Along with other skills like reading ahead, striving to never stop while reading (to prevent getting lost), and becoming more relaxed while playing and reading with confidence, you've come a long way in the previous 11 chapters.

In this final chapter, we'll challenge you with changes in the time signature that include both meter and beat unit changes. You'll need all the skills you've learned thus far to effectively read down these final passages. *All* Note Groups will be in the mix as well as many of the essential components examined in past chapters. Remember what you've learned, and be the reader—and player—you were meant to be.

Cut Time

The examples in this book have been set mainly in 4/4 and for good reason: It's the most commonly used time signature. It's also often referred to as *common time* and abbreviated in notation with a fancy-looking "C," like this:

Now, if you run a vertical line down through the center of that "C," thus "cutting" the time signature in half, 4/4 becomes 2/2, which is more commonly known as *cut time*.

While it has slightly different meanings among musicians, the cut-time symbol is a standard in written music. More often than not, it indicates a "two-beat" feel, and the tempo is generally fast and flowing. Of course, this changes note duration hierarchy, making the half note the beat unit, and, along with its related rests, making it the note that receives one beat.

Here's how cut time breaks down:

Whole note = 2 beats

Half note = 1 beat

Quarter note = 1/2 beat

Eighth note = 1/4 beat

Sixteenth note = 1/8 beat

The following passages will alternate from common time to cut time, but maintain the same melodies and notational rhythms. The cut time passages should be played the same as the common time passages, but feel twice as fast. The idea is to develop your rhythm recognition skills of duration with yet another beat unit and note duration hierarchy. With your metronome set somewhere between 50–65 bpm, be sure to keep track of the time signature shifts as you apply some of the recycling methods, such as reading in columns!

Odd Meters

We've firmly established 4/4 as the most common meter in music, with 3/4 and compound meters like 6/8 and 12/8 also very popular. But across myriad styles you'll occasionally find other meters with odd numbers on top, such as 5/4, 7/4, 11/8, or even as high as 15/8. One way to approach reading in these seemingly off-center feels is by looking for *recurring groupings*.

The above 5/4 passage has a 3-beat/2-beat pattern. The 5/4 time can also have a 2-beat/3-beat pattern, like this.

A good place to start putting this concept into practice is with the meters of 5/4 and 7/4, which is what you have in these final passages below. Be sure to key in on the aforementioned 5/4 groupings as well as the 4-beat/3-beat and 3-beat/4-beat groupings commonly found in 7/4. Within all these rhythmic grouping environments you'll find a lot of motivic writing. So keep an eye out for the motives listed at the end of Chapter 5.

By now, you know what to do with that metronome!

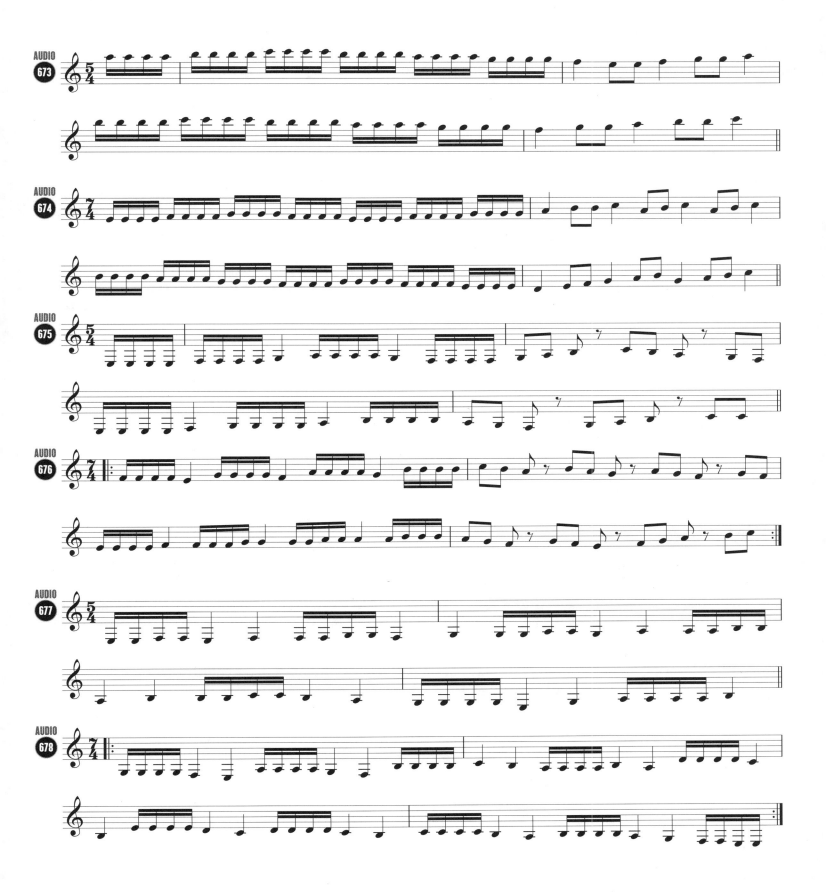

Final Words

Congratulations! You've made it through! I sincerely thank you for taking this journey with me, and I truly hope this book has served you well. The goal in writing this book was to teach skills that will enable guitarists to functionally read music in a relaxed yet commanding manner based on a solid understanding of what it is you're reading. But your job is far from complete. You need to maintain the skills that you've gained and strive to further them, and the only way to do that is to *read, read, read, and read some more!*

Reading—and playing for that matter—on any instrument is a lifelong journey. With the knowledge you've gained in this book, your journey will not only be smoother, but also more exciting than you ever imagined.

Get Better at Guitar

...with these Great Guitar Instruction Books from Hal Leonard!

101 GUITAR TIPS
INCLUDES TAB

STUFF ALL THE PROS KNOW AND USE

by Adam St. James

This book contains invaluable guidance on everything from scales and music theory to truss rod adjustments, proper recording studio set-ups, and much more. The book also features snippets of advice from some of the most celebrated guitarists and producers in the music business, including B.B. King, Steve Vai, Joe Satriani, Warren Haynes, Laurence Juber, Pete Anderson, Tom Dowd and others, culled from the author's hundreds of interviews.

00695737 Book/CD Pack.........................$16.95

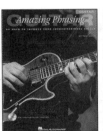

AMAZING PHRASING
INCLUDES TAB

50 WAYS TO IMPROVE YOUR IMPROVISATIONAL SKILLS

by Tom Kolb

This book/CD pack explores all the main components necessary for crafting well-balanced rhythmic and melodic phrases. It also explains how these phrases are put together to form cohesive solos. Many styles are covered – rock, blues, jazz, fusion, country, Latin, funk and more – and all of the concepts are backed up with musical examples. The companion CD contains 89 demos for listening, and most tracks feature full-band backing.

00695583 Book/CD Pack.........................$19.95

BLUES YOU CAN USE
INCLUDES TAB

by John Ganapes

A comprehensive source designed to help guitarists develop both lead and rhythm playing. Covers: Texas, Delta, R&B, early rock and roll, gospel, blues/rock and more. Includes: 21 complete solos • chord progressions and riffs • turnarounds • moveable scales and more. CD features leads and full band backing.

00695007 Book/CD Pack.........................$19.95

FRETBOARD MASTERY
INCLUDES TAB

by Troy Stetina

Untangle the mysterious regions of the guitar fretboard and unlock your potential. *Fretboard Mastery* familiarizes you with all the shapes you need to know by applying them in real musical examples, thereby reinforcing and reaffirming your newfound knowledge. The result is a much higher level of comprehension and retention.

00695331 Book/CD Pack.........................$19.95

FRETBOARD ROADMAPS – 2ND EDITION

ESSENTIAL GUITAR PATTERNS THAT ALL THE PROS KNOW AND USE

by Fred Sokolow

The updated edition of this bestseller features more songs, updated lessons, and a full audio CD! Learn to play lead and rhythm anywhere on the fretboard, in any key; play a variety of lead guitar styles; play chords and progressions anywhere on the fretboard; expand your chord vocabulary; and learn to think musically – the way the pros do.

00695941 Book/CD Pack.........................$14.95

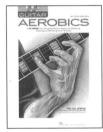

GUITAR AEROBICS
INCLUDES TAB

A 52-WEEK, ONE-LICK-PER-DAY WORKOUT PROGRAM FOR DEVELOPING, IMPROVING & MAINTAINING GUITAR TECHNIQUE

by Troy Nelson

From the former editor of *Guitar One* magazine, here is a daily dose of vitamins to keep your chops fine tuned! Musical styles include rock, blues, jazz, metal, country, and funk. Techniques taught include alternate picking, arpeggios, sweep picking, string skipping, legato, string bending, and rhythm guitar. These exercises will increase speed, and improve dexterity and pick- and fret-hand accuracy. The accompanying CD includes all 365 workout licks plus play-along grooves in every style at eight different metronome settings.

00695946 Book/CD Pack.........................$19.99

GUITAR CLUES
INCLUDES TAB

OPERATION PENTATONIC

by Greg Koch

Join renowned guitar master Greg Koch as he clues you in to a wide variety of fun and valuable pentatonic scale applications. Whether you're new to improvising or have been doing it for a while, this book/CD pack will provide loads of delicious licks and tricks that you can use right away, from volume swells and chicken pickin' to intervallic and chordal ideas. The CD includes 65 demo and play-along tracks.

00695827 Book/CD Pack.........................$19.95

INTRODUCTION TO GUITAR TONE & EFFECTS

by David M. Brewster

This book/CD pack teaches the basics of guitar tones and effects, with audio examples on CD. Readers will learn about: overdrive, distortion and fuzz • using equalizers • modulation effects • reverb and delay • multi-effect processors • and more.

00695766 Book/CD Pack.........................$14.99

PICTURE CHORD ENCYCLOPEDIA

This comprehensive guitar chord resource for all playing styles and levels features five voicings of 44 chord qualities for all twelve keys – 2,640 chords in all! For each, there is a clearly illustrated chord frame, as well as *an actual photo* of the chord being played! Includes info on basic fingering principles, open chords and barre chords, partial chords and broken-set forms, and more.

00695224...$19.95

SCALE CHORD RELATIONSHIPS
INCLUDES TAB

by Michael Mueller & Jeff Schroedl

This book teaches players how to determine which scales to play with which chords, so guitarists will never have to fear chord changes again! This book/CD pack explains how to: recognize keys • analyze chord progressions • use the modes • play over nondiatonic harmony • use harmonic and melodic minor scales • use symmetrical scales such as chromatic, whole-tone and diminished scales • incorporate exotic scales such as Hungarian major and Gypsy minor • and much more!

00695563 Book/CD Pack.........................$14.95

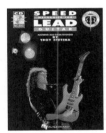

SPEED MECHANICS FOR LEAD GUITAR
INCLUDES TAB

Take your playing to the stratosphere with the most advanced lead book by this proven heavy metal author. *Speed Mechanics* is the ultimate technique book for developing the kind of speed and precision in today's explosive playing styles. Learn the fastest ways to achieve speed and control, secrets to make your practice time really count, and how to open your ears and make your musical ideas more solid and tangible. Packed with over 200 vicious exercises including Troy's scorching version of "Flight of the Bumblebee." Music and examples demonstrated on CD. 89-minute audio.

00699323 Book/CD Pack.........................$19.95

TOTAL ROCK GUITAR
INCLUDES TAB

A COMPLETE GUIDE TO LEARNING ROCK GUITAR

by Troy Stetina

This unique and comprehensive source for learning rock guitar is designed to develop both lead and rhythm playing. It covers: getting a tone that rocks • open chords, power chords and barre chords • riffs, scales and licks • string bending, strumming, palm muting, harmonics and alternate picking • all rock styles • and much more. The examples are in standard notation with chord grids and tab, and the CD includes full-band backing for all 22 songs.

00695246 Book/CD Pack.........................$19.99

MUSICIANS INSTITUTE PRESS is the official series of Southern California's renowned music school, Musicians Institute. MI instructors, some of the finest musicians in the world, share their vast knowledge and experience with you – no matter what your current level. For guitar, bass, drums, vocals, and keyboards, MI Press offers the finest music curriculum for higher learning through a variety of series:

ESSENTIAL CONCEPTS	**MASTER CLASS**	**PRIVATE LESSONS**
Designed from MI core curriculum programs.	Designed from MI elective courses.	Tackle a variety of topics "one-on one" with MI faculty instructors.

GUITAR

Acoustic Artistry
by Evan Hirschelman • Private Lessons
00695922 Book/CD Pack $19.99

Advanced Guitar Soloing
by Daniel Gilbert & Beth Marlis • Essential Concepts
00695636 Book/CD Pack $19.99

Advanced Scale Concepts & Licks for Guitar
by Jean Marc Belkadi • Private Lessons
00695298 Book/CD Pack $16.95

Basic Blues Guitar
by Steve Trovato • Private Lessons
00695180 Book/CD Pack $15.99

Blues/Rock Soloing for Guitar
by Robert Calva • Private Lessons
00695680 Book/CD Pack $19.99

Blues Rhythm Guitar
by Keith Wyatt • Master Class
00695131 Book/CD Pack $19.95

Dean Brown
00696002 DVD $29.95

Chord Progressions for Guitar
by Tom Kolb • Private Lessons
00695664 Book/CD Pack $17.99

Chord Tone Soloing
by Barrett Tagliarino • Private Lessons
00695855 Book/CD Pack $24.99

Chord-Melody Guitar
by Bruce Buckingham • Private Lessons
00695646 Book/CD Pack $17.99

Classical & Fingerstyle Guitar Techniques
by David Oakes • Master Class
00695171 Book/CD Pack $17.99

Classical Themes for Electric Guitar
by Jean Marc Belkadi • Private Lessons
00695806 Book/CD Pack $15.99

Contemporary Acoustic Guitar
by Eric Paschal & Steve Trovato • Master Class
00695320 Book/CD Pack $16.95

Creative Chord Shapes
by Jamie Findlay • Private Lessons
00695172 Book/CD Pack $10.99

Diminished Scale for Guitar
by Jean Marc Belkadi • Private Lessons
00695227 Book/CD Pack $10.99

Essential Rhythm Guitar
by Steve Trovato • Private Lessons
00695181 Book/CD Pack $15.99

Ethnic Rhythms for Electric Guitar
by Jean Marc Belkadi • Private Lessons
00695873 Book/CD Pack $17.99

Exotic Scales & Licks for Electric Guitar
by Jean Marc Belkadi • Private Lessons
00695860 Book/CD Pack $16.95

Funk Guitar
by Ross Bolton • Private Lessons
00695419 Book/CD Pack $15.99

Guitar Basics
by Bruce Buckingham • Private Lessons
00695134 Book/CD Pack $17.95

Guitar Fretboard Workbook
by Barrett Tagliarino • Essential Concepts
00695712 . . . . $19.99

Guitar Hanon
by Peter Deneff • Private Lessons
00695321 . . . . $9.95

Guitar Lick•tionary
by Dave Hill • Private Lessons
00695482 Book/CD Pack $19.99

Guitar Soloing
by Dan Gilbert & Beth Marlis • Essential Concepts
00695190 Book/CD Pack $22.99
00695907 DVD $19.95

Harmonics
by Jamie Findlay • Private Lessons
00695169 Book/CD Pack $13.99

Introduction to Jazz Guitar Soloing
by Joe Elliott • Master Class
00695406 Book/CD Pack $19.95

Jazz Guitar Chord System
by Scott Henderson • Private Lessons
00695291 . . . . $10.95

Jazz Guitar Improvisation
by Sid Jacobs • Master Class
00695128 Book/CD Pack $18.99
00695908 DVD $19.95
00695639 VHS Video $19.95

Jazz-Rock Triad Improvising
by Jean Marc Belkadi • Private Lessons
00695361 Book/CD Pack $15.99

Latin Guitar
by Bruce Buckingham • Master Class
00695379 Book/CD Pack $17.99

Liquid Legato
by Allen Hinds • Private Lessons
00696656 Book/CD Pack $14.99

Modern Approach to Jazz, Rock & Fusion Guitar
by Jean Marc Belkadi • Private Lessons
00695143 Book/CD Pack $15.99

Modern Jazz Concepts for Guitar
by Sid Jacobs • Master Class
00695711 Book/CD Pack $16.95

Modern Rock Rhythm Guitar
by Danny Gill • Private Lessons
00695682 Book/CD Pack $16.95

Modes for Guitar
by Tom Kolb • Private Lessons
00695555 Book/CD Pack $18.99

Music Reading for Guitar
by David Oakes • Essential Concepts
00695192 . . . . $19.99

The Musician's Guide to Recording Acoustic Guitar
by Dallan Beck • Private Lessons
00695505 Book/CD Pack $13.99

Outside Guitar Licks
by Jean Marc Belkadi • Private Lessons
00695697 Book/CD Pack $16.99

Power Plucking
by Dale Turner • Private Lesson
00695962 . . . . $19.95

Practice Trax for Guitar
by Danny Gill • Private Lessons
00695601 Book/CD Pack $17.99

Progressive Tapping Licks
by Jean Marc Belkadi • Private Lessons
00695748 Book/CD Pack $15.95

Rhythm Guitar
by Bruce Buckingham & Eric Paschal • Essential Concepts
00695188 Book $17.95
00114559 Book/CD Pack $24.99
00695909 DVD $19.95

Rhythmic Lead Guitar
by Barrett Tagliarino • Private Lessons
00110263 Book/CD Pack $19.99

Rock Lead Basics
by Nick Nolan & Danny Gill • Master Class
00695144 Book/CD Pack $18.99
00695910 DVD $19.95

Rock Lead Performance
by Nick Nolan & Danny Gill • Master Class
00695278 Book/CD Pack $17.95

Rock Lead Techniques
by Nick Nolan & Danny Gill • Master Class
00695146 Book/CD Pack $16.99

Shred Guitar
by Greg Harrison • Master Class
00695977 Book/CD Pack $19.99

Slap & Pop Technique for Guitar
00695645 Book/CD Pack $14.99

Technique Exercises for Guitar
by Jean Marc Belkadi • Private Lessons
00695913 . . . . $15.99

Texas Blues Guitar
by Robert Calva • Private Lessons
00695340 Book/CD Pack $17.95

Ultimate Guitar Technique
by Bill LaFleur • Private Lessons
00695863 . . . . $22.99

Prices, contents, and availability subject to change without notice.

7777 W. BLUEMOUND RD. P.O. BOX 13819 MILWAUKEE, WI 53213
www.halleonard.com